THE CARDINALS OF
COBLEIGH MANOR

This book is a sequel to:

Wendy of Glendorran
At the King's Command

THE CARDINALS OF COBLEIGH MANOR

By
P. CATHERINE COLES

VICTORY PRESS
LONDON

Printed in Great Britain for
Victory Press, Clapham Crescent, London, S.W.4
by Richard Clay and Company Ltd., Bungay, Suffolk

CHAPTER ONE

INTRODUCING THE FAMILY

THE sharp burr burr of the telephone bell sounded clearly up the staircase of Cobleigh Manor and penetrated into the nursery, a room suddenly silent after the merry bedtime fun. Wendy pushed back her dishevelled hair, took a last look at the sleeping children, and ran downstairs to answer it. The 'phone always seemed extra busy on Marylin's night off.

Wendy was not at all surprised to recognise the voice of her old school-friend, Mollie Ridelle, on the 'phone. Since her illness three years previously she had kept in close touch with the family and had been a not infrequent visitor at the Manor. Invariably if she were in town she would call Wendy on the 'phone, and the many miles between her home in Glasgow and Cobleigh were spanned by a very regular exchange of chatty letters. Tonight was different. Mollie was far nearer than a hotel in London; she was at Cobleigh railway station, begging an hour with Wendy that very evening. From the tone of her voice her business was urgent and serious.

"But of course come out, Mollie, and you'll stay the night; so don't go booking a room in the hotel!"

Wendy laughed. She knew Mollie well enough to know that she would never impose on her friends, who had no intention of letting her sleep under any roof but their own.

"You are a dear, Wendy! I was going to leave my case and book a room before coming along. Are you sure it's convenient?"

"Absolutely. Christopher is out at some Young Farmers' Club, speaking about something or other edifying, and the others will all be busy with their own affairs until late, so we shall be just our two selves and can have a grand talk over dinner."

Mollie rang off, and Wendy hurried away to prepare Cook for Mollie's arrival, and to put a bowl of roses into the charming spare room that stood always ready for use at a moment's notice. As Wendy left the kitchen she reflected on what a joy it was now to have her staff rallying round her, making it so easy for them to keep the kind of "open house" of the Manor that they had wanted from the first—a haven for any, friend or stranger, in time of trouble or need of any kind. And what a steady stream of folk they had had, but Mollie had been the first, and it had been her obvious response to their kindness that had opened the way for others to follow on.

Looking back over the years, Wendy marvelled at how things had turned out: not only so different from their hopes and expectations, but so much better. She checked herself—did she really mean that? Had all that had happened in the past few years been better than her dreams?

"You are looking thoughtful, Wendy!" The cheery voice of her cousin, Lindsey Harris, broke across her reverie and brought her back to the present moment.

Wendy smiled.

"I caught myself thinking that things had all turned out so much better for us than we had planned for ourselves, and I was just wondering if that was really my honest summing up of it all."

"And it is? You looked as if you were coming to some such conclusion."

"Yes; you know Christopher and I wanted to use the Manor to help people like Mollie, and I often think now that God has done that indirectly, and on a wider scale than we could foresee. When Paul got polio and it was so wonderful to know we could have him home quite quickly because of your skill and willingness to care for him, it seemed as if our earlier plan was not to be, but now——" Wendy spread her hands significantly towards the downstairs dormitory, where Paul no longer needed to sleep but which still sheltered seven other little polio victims in varying stages of recovery, cared for by the faithful Lindsey and their friend and ex-schoolfellow, June Raygold, who had trained with Lindsey at the same hospital. "Now we can not only help these wee scraps but we have a link with their parents : people we would never have met in the ordinary course of our lives. Only this afternoon Mrs. Wilson was here seeing her John, and she has quite stopped feeling resentful towards God about the boy's illness, and Christopher said that last time Mr. Wilson came he was much more ready for a talk. It'll be wonderful if Johnny's illness brings that family through to being the Lord's."

Lindsey nodded understandingly. She had watched it all take place. She had known of the success that had come after the long struggle to wrest Mollie from her despair, and she had marvelled at the transformation when Mollie finally yielded to the Lord. She had shared, too, in their longing that others should benefit by finding rest and sanctuary and spiritual adjustment in the delightful Manor House and garden that had lost its tawdry glitter and brittle social atmosphere under its new master and mistress. And she had been the first to hear the news of little Paul's grave illness two years previously, just when he seemed to be such a sturdy toddler and so thrilled and proud at the advent of his baby sister Elspeth. Then it was that she had silently and without any fuss relinquished her post as Matron at Glendorran, gone back to hospital for a refresher course, and arrived at Cobleigh prepared to take charge of Paul, fully equipped to give him all the latest polio treatment.

The present phase of life at the Manor had somehow grown out of that gesture of Lindsey's made so spontaneously to help her cousin, to whom she always felt so indebted for all that life had come to be to her. The Cardinals were able to fit up a room with a good deal of equipment that could mean much to hastening Paul's recovery, and it was the knowledge of this that spurred them all on with the idea that other children might share what Paul could have so easily provided for him. Their family doctor jumped at the idea, and in no time at all was in touch with the specialists visiting two children's hospitals. Before three months were out, Lindsey, to her huge satisfaction, found herself in charge of seven small patients and grateful for June's timely offer to help. All that left Wendy free to care for baby Elspeth and the rest of the home and the estate and all that went into making her life and Christopher's so busy and useful.

Wendy glanced at her watch.

"Well, I mustn't day-dream. That was Mollie on the 'phone. She's at Cobleigh Station and coming out for the night. I gather she has some pressing problem."

"Oh, good, I'm glad she's coming again. I'm off to Granny Cardinal's for a couple of hours. June's getting the bairns to sleep."

"Collect her on your way back and come in for a last cup of tea before you turn in. Christopher will be back later, and Mollie will have had time to unburden herself of whatever is weighing heavily upon her—we'll have a jolly Dormy reunion!"

"Good-oh! Jam tarts and all?"

Lindsey laughed wickedly and departed before Wendy could answer.

Wendy went to the sitting-room and tidied the cushions. How far away those Fourth Form days seemed now, though sometimes she felt the years slipping by so quickly. Perhaps that was because all the old bunch from the Dormitory had managed to keep in touch, and when they were together, as they would be tonight, time had a way of rolling back. They would recount the endless "do you remembers" and enter once more the happy realm of their schoolgirl days.

Within the next few minutes Mollie's taxi drew up at the door of Cobleigh Manor and, simultaneously, Lindsey was tapping at the friendly open door of the Dower House and being welcomed into the wide window-seat of the sunny living-room. Christopher's mother had changed with the years, and never wearied of telling, with an eager light in her eyes, how that change had come about.

Her first months of living at the Dower House had not been easy. Though it had been her own choice to go there and leave the young couple free to use the Manor as they might wish, she had given way to many hours of regret and self-pity. This was what happened when you got old and a widow, she told herself, the young people preferred your room to your company. But she knew it wasn't true, she knew she could have been wanted if she had taken the trouble to be a little more lovable. And then her friends had considered her foolish and weak to make the change, and had not hesitated to tell her so. Some who had enjoyed frequent visits to the Manor were far less ready to call at the little Dower House that stood at a short distance up a winding path behind the Manor House, nicely furnished though it was within. Then there had been staff difficulties. Betty, her personal maid, had felt the change in status keenly. To her there was all the difference in the world between the Manor House and the Dower House, and she made unreasonable demands on her mistress to compensate her injured feelings. When she found these were not to be met she left in high dudgeon. Marylin found the new maid, a cheery, good-natured girl, but though she and her mistress suited each other perfectly now, there had been stormy scenes at the beginning.

But the real change had come just about the time Elspeth was born. One afternoon, Paul, to his great glee, was bundled up unceremoniously by Marylin and dumped at his granny's and told that for a great treat he would be allowed to spend the night all by himself with his granny. This was a wonderful new venture for the child, who had early discovered the softest spot in the heart that could never remain austere and abrupt with the little grandson.

Marylin deposited her young charge thankfully and hurried away to the bustling activity of the Manor. Paul and his granny settled down companionably to the well-spread tea-table. Granny poured out his milk and put a buttered scone on to his plate. Two large eyes watched her incredulously.

"You haven't said 'Thank-You' to God, Granny," he said in simple wonderment as she urged him to begin.

Granny was taken aback. Of course, on the few occasions that she allowed herself to accept the young people's invitation to a meal at the Manor her son did ask a blessing, but she had never made a habit of it herself. But as she looked at Paul, she knew she had met her match : that child would never eat one mouthful without the proper preliminary, nor could he be put off with a hastily prepared excuse.

"Oh, I forgot!" The words slipped out automatically. Then she had an idea. "Suppose you say 'Thank-You' for both of us, Paul?" she asked hopefully.

Paul shut his eyes and folded his little hands.

"Dear Lord Jesus, Thank-You for this very nice tea we are going to have, and Thank-You for Granny having me to stay tonight in her nice home—and please don't mind her having forgotten to say Thank-You herself, she was busy thinking about me, but she'll 'member next time. Amen."

Calmly and undisturbed by the incident, Paul now settled happily to his scones and butter and honey, and to Granny's famous chocolate sponge cake, that was ever a favourite with him, but his granny had a problem. True enough, she had forgotten what would be expected of her, but that was not by any means the only forgotten memory. Moreover, Paul would not expect her to forget again, and Lady Cardinal had not wanted to remember about God, not for many, many years now. Could she "ask her blessing" for the sake of her grandson and go on ignoring God in her own heart at the same time? Common honesty told her she could not.

That night, after Paul was asleep, the Dower House was very still. A tired, troubled old lady who had so deliberately set herself against the gentle, gracious love of God through many long years of social climbing, got humbly down on her knees and sought Him for herself. And because her seeking was in earnest and because the Good Shepherd is always looking for His lost sheep and listening for their least cry, that night she found her way to life, and to the joy and peace that come to those who love and trust the Saviour. It was with the light of this new experience in her eyes—eyes that had been wet with tears during that same evening—that she turned to meet her son when she heard his quick step on the path outside.

Christopher had strode light-heartedly up the little path to tell his mother that she now had a grand-daughter as well as a grandson, and he went home not many minutes later with the added joy of knowing that at last his mother, too, was one with them in the things that mattered most.

An entirely new and happy phase of life began in the old Dower House, and it was to this peaceful home that Lindsey liked to turn at the end of a busy day.

CHAPTER TWO

GLENDORRAN REUNION

OVER dinner that night Mollie and Wendy chatted about all manner of things, filling the gap in their news of each other in the weeks since their last exchange of letters. Then, quite suddenly, over their coffee, Mollie came to the point of her visit. Monica O'Riley, her niece, was in trouble. All her childhood, Monica's parents had been abroad, and Mollie had filled the role of guardian as well as aunt. On leaving Glendorran two years previously, Monica had taken a course at a Domestic Science College and made a good success of it. Then in September she had taken her first post and become the Matron of a very fashionable co-educational boarding-school. Mollie had had reservations about this wonderful opening that had so thrilled her niece. True, she was ambitious for her to get on, and, as Monica insisted, such schools needed Christian matrons quite as much as schools like Glendorran. With that argument Mollie was silenced, but not satisfied. Now she had another story to tell.

After less than two terms Monica had been asked to leave St. Adrian's. To her aunt she had been reticent about the true reason, merely shrugging her shoulders and saying that the head considered her unsuitable, but Mollie had made it her business to investigate below the surface. If Mr. Johnson was being unreasonable, then Monica should at least be given longer notice or a second chance. But Mollie had only stirred up the mud. Monica had been given a second chance and a third chance, and had been reprimanded again and again for her behaviour.

"To make matters worse," Mollie went on, pouring out her tale into Wendy's sympathetic ear, "without a word to me or to her parents, the little monkey took herself over to Paris in January and saw James. I had to take her up on that, but she only said that our separation did not affect her relationship to us both, and he was still her uncle as much as I was her aunt. Of course, she's right in a way, and I blame myself because I used to be glad enough to leave her to him in the school holidays when I didn't want to be tied to the home on her account. They always got on well together."

Wendy listened, letting Mollie go on without interruption. She could understand how her friend was feeling. The old hard Mollie, who had clamoured only for wealth and position and had married unhappily in her struggle to gain her ambition, had given her niece a roof and the necessities of food and clothing, but not a home and no worthwhile training in those early, impressionable years. Wendy sighed. Small wonder if Mollie felt badly now. Monica's attitude was but the fruit of careless sowing, and yet they had all hoped better things of the child. At fifteen she had yielded to the claims of the Lord Jesus Christ and had taken a fine stand for Him, becoming the leader of the Christian Union both at Glendorran and, later, at College. Wendy had shared Mollie's doubts about St. Adrian's at the time and had been aware of certain signs of weakness in Monica's character that boded ill for her unless she set herself to keep to the highest path she knew.

"Where is she now?" Wendy asked, and Mollie, who had been staring wistfully out of the window as she admitted her failure with the girl, turned to her friend, with a troubled look in her eyes.

"That's the worst bit, Wendy. I don't know. She left St. Adrian's at half-term and came home, naturally enough, and I got part of the true story from her. Then—oh, I suppose I was foolish, but she seems so immature and I am her guardian—I tried to talk to her and persuade her into better ways, and she made it quite clear that such interference was quite unforgivable. My lady reminded me that she was of age, and there and then packed her suitcase and left the house."

"Oh, Mollie, I am sorry! When was that?"

"Tuesday."

"And this is Friday. Has she left no address?"

"None."

"Would she go to James again, do you think?"

"I wondered that, but I've no way of finding out. It's—well, it's a matter of years now since I wrote to James. Just that one letter when I reopened the Glasgow home, and he never answered. I can't write now; at least, not yet."

"N-no." Wendy spoke slowly and thoughtfully.

"I was remembering just now that bit I came to love so much in Hudson Taylor's life—when he learned to reach other people through God. I discovered it first when we were having such trouble with Granny Cardinal. Do you remember I told you what a real thrill it was to reach people by prayer instead of blundering in myself and doing the wrong thing?"

Mollie smiled.

"I do remember, and I've often thought that must have been the way you reached me, so I know how effective it can be. If you and Christopher had 'dealt with me', I doubt if I would be where I am today. I think I made just that mistake. I cornered Monica and lectured her, from her point of view, and no matter how right my motive seemed to me, she could not see it that way. Why ever didn't I remember what you'd done for me?"

"It's not too late, my dear. Look—stay on with us over the week-end and we'll really get down to some definite prayer for Monica. Besides, you've June and Lindsey to meet; they will be coming in for our evening cup of tea soon, and you must get to know all our little patients, too, tomorrow. My first reaction to your news was to invite Monica here, but I can see that she would never come in her present mood, she would smell innumerable rats ! But Mollie, don't feel that it is hopeless. God has His own far better plan for her recovery, and we can serve Him and her best by being open to see His way and follow it. Now, what about a walk to see the roses before the others join us? I'll just slip upstairs and see that my two are sound asleep—I won't be a minute."

The two friends got up, and as Wendy went up-stairs Mollie wandered out through the hall on to the rose-fragrant terrace. She sighed, and the sigh was a mixture of contentment and trouble. Cobleigh Manor and its mistress meant so much to her. She thought back to the days when she had so resented Wendy's jolly life that was unobtrusively marked out by an integrity that would not stoop to the mean or dis-honest act. On through the years, Wendy had stead-fastly chosen the best and weathered the storms in her quest for the highest, yet ever willing to wait and reach out a hand to a floundering Mollie, had she been ready to take it instead of content to play in the shallows and chase moonshine and worthless trifles, finding for herself only bitterness of soul. And it had been Wendy who had lifted her out of those sordid depths when, ultimately, she had reached the end of herself and been ready only to sink.

"That's them asleep!"

Wendy laughed, heedless of her grammar as she joined her friend.

It was a perfect night, and the garden was gay with all the colour of early June. The rockery, the rose-garden, the borders lined with refreshing pinks, the carnations, the honeysuckled arbour, the lily-pond : all had to be visited, and because Wendy knew and loved them all so much she could make her pleasure in them spill over to her visitor. For a while, at least, in that quiet garden, surrounded by the magic of colour and fragrance, their ears tuned to the hum of the bee and the twitter of young birds in the evening sunshine, Monica and her waywardness began to burden her aunt a little less for the first time in many weeks.

A softly called "coo-ee!" across the lawn turned their steps towards the house once more and heralded the arrival of June and Lindsey. Soon the four Old Glendorians were companionably ensconced in comfortable deck-chairs on the terrace.

"One really nice point in favour of Cobleigh Manor, I always think!" Lindsey said slowly, as she lay back, her hands linked behind her head.

"What's that?"

"A noticeable and most attractive absence of midges!"

The others laughed.

"Do you remember the little brutes at tennis practices? You had to wave your racquet twice round your head between every stroke to keep them away!" June joined in.

"Yes, and the poor onlookers had a frightful time —no racquets to wave, and we got shouted at for putting the players off their stroke if we jumped about too much. Still it was worth a few midges to watch old Wendy on the courts, I must say."

"I was no star. It seems so funny now to think of the serious young army officer cadet, Christopher Cardinal, coaching a leggy schoolgirl in this very garden!"

"I often wondered if he saw beyond the schoolgirl

even then," Mollie said quietly. "He never seems to have looked in any other direction."

Wendy had a soft, far-away look in her eyes as she answered. She smiled at Mollie—Mollie who knew what it was to be looked past and turned from.

"He always says he made up his mind the first day he saw me. I suppose he knows. To me he was just a very kind person to bother his head with a school kid, and I was as much in awe of him as of his parents, although it was much easier to talk to him when I found he was the Lord's. I certainly never had any day-dreams of being the Lady of the Manor, I can tell you!"

The four friends sat silent for a moment, and then came that sudden upsurge of "do you remembers" that carried them back over the years to one incident after another. Slowly they gathered up many loose threads as each had news of one and another of their old schoolfellows, and by the time Christopher came home they were indeed a bunch of schoolgirls once again, calling the staff by their nicknames and chaffing each other over the varied reminiscences.

At the sound of her husband's car in the drive Wendy excused herself to her guests and left them to chatter on. When she returned, Christopher was with her, and close behind came Marylin pushing a well-spread tea-trolley.

When Mollie was ready to get into bed that night she drew back the curtains and looked out. She hated to miss a moment of early morning sunshine, and she guessed she would not rouse easily after her day's travelling. Outside the garden was silent save for the distant, eerie hoot of an owl. Everywhere was white with brilliant moonlight. She stood, spellbound, watching, listening, drinking in the beauty, the majesty, the magnificence of the scene, letting its wonder possess her and fill her with a great stillness. For days now she had been battling with Monica, battling with her problem. She felt as if she had been in the midst of a fierce thunderstorm, and now the storm was over and it was calm. She dropped on her knees beside the open window. True, Monica was not found yet, nor was she turned into wiser and safer ways, but the peace that had gone from Mollie's heart was restored, and with that tranquillity came a new sense of trust and a new desire to pray.

CHAPTER THREE

INDEPENDENCE

WHEN Monica walked indignantly out of her aunt's flat she had no clear-cut plan formed in her mind. She only knew that she was of age and was not going to be lectured by her bossy aunt any longer. She thought of Uncle James in Paris. She could be certain of a welcome from him and no reprimands. In fact, he would enjoy siding with her and finding fault with Aunt Mollie's stuffy Victorian ideals. But somehow Monica did not really want to go to Uncle James and enlist disloyal sympathy against her aunt. In January she had gone in a mood of sudden bravado, knowing full well that she was not expected to go to him now and the experience had held no real happiness for her. Uncle James had been good to her, but she did not much like his friends, and all the time she was there she felt a bit mean towards Aunt Mollie. Of course, her aunt deserved it, Monica sternly told herself; she wasn't going back on that trip, but she did not think it would be wise to repeat it. Even so, if her aunt would interfere with her young niece's life, well, maybe she would need to be reminded, just occasionally, that she could not afford to throw too many stones at other people, even yet.

All those thoughts had marched rather majestic-

ally through the girl's mind as she had been packing
her suitcase and walking out of the house with a
fine show of injured dignity. It was quite another
matter to be out on one's own with a not-too-glowing
reference in one's possession and very little experience behind one.

On leaving the house, Monica had taken a bus
into town and was now sitting well hidden in a recess
of a tea-shop sipping hot coffee and wondering what
to do next. She dismissed Uncle James without
further consideration. There were school and college
friends : they were mostly well occupied with their
own affairs, though not a few homes in the district
would have opened their doors willingly enough to
the keen Monica of former days when prayer meet-
ings, youth squashes and such events took her from
home to home amongst her equally keen companions.
Now she could picture the scandalised look on some
faces if she made an appearance in her present mood
with anything but a "success story" to explain her
situation.

The waitress hovered near.

"Cheque, Miss?"

Monica started guiltily. She had not realised how
long she had been sitting there, nor that the deserted
tea-room was now thronging with the lunch-hour
crowds. She pulled herself together. A merry, laughing bunch of office girls came in and took possession
of her table. Their light-heartedness was infectious.
Her own spirits began to rise. After all, she was
young and she had a big enough allowance from her

parents to pay her way at the moment. She would make a go of life all right and prove to the dreary old fogies that her ways were as good as theirs. She took out her purse and paid her bill. She tossed back her hatless head of pretty brown curls and left the tea-shop more jauntily than she had entered it, a new plan forming in her adventurous mind.

Over in the station she scanned the train-destination board hopefully. The midday Scot to London called at Crewe; there was a train for Edinburgh; two local trains leaving almost at once; another for the West coast—the old familiar Glendorran journey.

The minute hand of the giant station clock jumped on remorselessly. She must decide quickly. A thought flashed into her mind. How did one make a momentous decision? The toss of a coin? Her whole future could lie cradled in the next step she might take. Memory stirred. Less than a year ago she would have prayed for guidance. She smiled cynically to herself. She had stopped praying. The staff room at St. Adrian's had buzzed with discussions and arguments on religious opinions, and by general consent prayer had been written off as nice for children and harmlessly soothing for the old and ill. Monica was not old or ill, and had no wish to be thought childish. She turned from the memory. Her life was her own affair. Her parents had left her to the tender mercies of an inefficient relative, and now that she was old enough to know her own mind that same aunt was beginning to throw her weight about and trying, quite unreasonably, to become efficient. Well, it was too late now. Another minute jumped by. There was no time to lose. Acting on sudden impulse, Monica rushed to the booking-office and hurriedly bought a single ticket to London. She ran on to the platform and was bundled, unceremoniously, into the last carriage by an indignant porter who muttered about thoughtless young people who risked their lives and other people's. The train was pulling out. Monica paused in the corridor long enough to regain her breath and put away purse and ticket. Then she gathered up her belongings and began to hunt for a seat.

The train was crowded, and she journeyed through several carriages before she spotted a vacant place. She began to push the sliding door of the compartment and then realised that the carriage held only one occupant, though bags and coats were spread out in confusion over most of the seats. That one occupant was a man, his head buried in the depths of the daily paper, his feet resting untidily on the opposite seat. She hesitated, wondering whether to try farther up the train. She was too late. Her touch on the door made the man look up. At once he tossed the paper aside, sprang up and came to her assistance.

"Why, Monique! This is wonderful!"

Monica drew back. Basil, of all people—a boy she had not met since the last of the old, unhappy holidays in the deserted Glasgow home; a son of one of Uncle James' friends.

It was no use protesting. Basil had silently taken

her case and her coat, and already had them stowed
away on the rack. Monica surveyed the seating. It
was a compartment for six, and it seemed as if there
were four missing travelling companions, judging
by the coats and cases. She hesitated. She supposed
the vacant seat was in the corner opposite Basil.

"Better come and sit next to me, Monique. All
this clutter belongs to three dreadful old girls who
have gone for lunch, and I think on their return
they will withdraw to the seats farthest removed from
the detestable young man they found here on their
arrival—that's me, Monique!" The boy grinned
impishly. "When they come back we'll go for lunch.
My high I.Q. told me that these old ducks would
like my absence better than my company, so I let
them go to first lunch, planning to put off the hour
of making their more intimate acquaintance as long
as possible—I assure you the feelings are mutual—
and now this stroke of luck: The beautiful Monique
to lunch with me."

He spoke possessively.

Monica felt helpless. She knew she ought to speak
sharply to this boy, make him behave himself and,
failing that, take her things and depart to another
compartment. But the silvery music of his "Monique" captivated her. Always, all her life, to everyone, she had been "Monica": a name she hated for
its hard matter-of-factness. But Basil made her name
sound so different, and she stifled her instinctive dis-
may at being in such a predicament. After all, it
was only for a journey, and Basil's "three old

girls'' would be back any minute, and they sounded exactly like the sort of suitable chaperon her aunt would have chosen for her.

By now Basil was pulling her down at his side and preparing to enjoy the rest of the journey thoroughly. The three came back, frowned at Basil and his companion and, as he had said, withdrew themselves as far as possible to the other end of the compartment. Basil squeezed Monica's hand knowingly.

"Lunch, honey?"

And with that same air of possession he piloted her out of the chaos and escorted her down the corridor to the dining-car. Monica's last twinge of conscience was stilled. This was fun, and she meant to enjoy every minute of it. Basil was a nice enough boy, and why shouldn't she be friendly with him? Uncle James had introduced them in the first place, and seemed to know his people well. Her visit to Paris, too, had taught her not to read anything more than common courtesy into the civilities of the many young men she met in her uncle's company, and she had behaved so well there among them that Uncle James had commented on it and been pleased for her to meet his friends.

It was most disappointing to find that Basil would leave the train at Crewe and go on from there to Birmingham, but as they sat together back in their compartment he asked her endless questions about her plans for the future and voted the Head of St. Adrian's a mean spoil sport to have been so hard on her.

As the train began to slacken its pace outside Crewe Basil took out his wallet and jotted down a name and address on a card, handing it over to Monica.

"This is my sister—my twin—she's a grand girl. Go to her, and she'll get you fixed up. She runs a youth hostel, and she gets to know about decent posts and things like that, too. Tell her I sent you, I'd like to think you were there—my Monique."

The last two words were spoken softly. The train jolted to a standstill. A last hand squeeze. A last word. Basil grabbed his case and was gone. The three looked at each other with ill-suppressed irritation and shut the door more firmly. Monica turned away from them and looked out of the window at the now darkening evening sky. With the going of Basil she felt desperately alone. She glanced at the name and address on the card and slipped it into her bag.

Should she go? She did not know. What was Basil's circle like? she wondered. Would his sister wonder at a girl turning up out of the blue on her brother's recommendation, or did he make a habit of it? Would his sister resent her arrival? Or, worse still, would she be patronising? That stiffened Monica. Determined to paddle her own canoe, she decided to go straight to the small private hotel at which she had stayed on previous visits to London, and wait and see what the new day might bring. She could always go to Basil's sister later.

With her mind made up, she leaned back and

closed her eyes. What a day it had been! Her thoughts drifted idly through its happenings until she reached the morning scene with her aunt. She opened her eyes suddenly and sat up, fumbling for Basil's discarded paper. Print of any kind to distract her was better than thinking now about Aunt Mollie.

The train roared on its way, and eventually Monica gathered up her belongings and was soon walking, as briskly as the crowded platform permitted, to hail a taxi and establish herself at the hotel.

B

CHAPTER FOUR

FRESH FIELDS

THE bright sunshine of a June morning stirred all the energy and vigour in Monica with new hope and new determination. After a most delicious breakfast she set off for a day in town, shopping and sightseeing, her cares thrown to the winds and only the thrill of her newly acquired independence controlling her. She mixed freely with the surging crowds in Oxford Street, dodged traffic light-heartedly and joined in the jostling throng who knew where to go for good food. With a deliberate act she closed her eye to the hole she was making in her allowance. She would get a job in a day or two, and for today she would be reckless and have her fling.

It was not until evening, after dinner in the hotel, that she idly picked up a ladies' magazine. She turned the pages casually, her mind really at work on another question: should she stay in and read, or should she go out and see what there was to be seen? She wasn't in the mood for fiction, her own life was too real and too exciting. She glanced at the trade advertisements: many of the goods she had already seen on display in the shops. Recipes and dress patterns had become part of her job, and she was on holiday just now and not interested. She came to the pages of vacant situations, and glanced

down the column. Really, what odd things some
people wanted! Her curiosity was roused. She read
on.

"Gentlewoman of integrity wanted"—she did not
think she would suit that. "Norway"—that sounded
interesting. "Fare paid and ample pocket money,
swimming and boating, suit younger person fond of
children." Vague, but rather fascinating if all else
failed. "Young girl, responsible, trustworthy, to give
help in busy home, hospitality and remuneration
offered, farm and country life, ample eggs, butter,
and milk." Well really! Monica smiled. She waded
on down the lists. Everyone wanted cheerful willing
service; some boldly stated the difficulties, some
bribed with promises of good wages, plenty of free
time, private bathrooms, bed-sitters, and wireless
sets, one stated baldly "two young boys under con-
trol of governess". That sounded like Alsatians
rather than children. She wondered what kind of a
dragon the governess might be. Then she came on it.
There it was in print, calling out to her.

"Wanted immediately, vacancy due to illness,
Domestic Science trained housekeeper to take full
responsibility for catering in recognised Children's
Home. Ample staff. Resident or non-resident by
arrangement. Happy atmosphere. Salary according
to approved scale. Temporary. Urgent. 'Phone: H—
4321."

Monica read and reread the words. It was ideal.
Temporary: that gave her time to look round, and
yet she would be earning and gaining experience.

Resident or non-resident: she had no second thoughts about that. She hated the restrictions of resident staff, they were too available for odd duties. And the urgency would mean that if only she could get an interview and please her prospective employer there would be no time to dig deeply into the deficiencies of the past. Her diploma was a good one, and the personal reference from the College had also been very much in her favour. She studied the paper again. She would 'phone at once. And then, as if to clinch the matter in her own mind, she noticed the 'phone number properly for the first time. It was the same exchange as that of Basil's sister. That meant she could get fixed up with job and hostel, just as simply as that. With never a doubt in her mind, she seized her bag and went out to the 'phone box in the hall.

Half an hour later, with all the confidence of youth, she was fixed up with an interview at the Home at ten o'clock the following morning. Very casually she had said she could start right away if she found it suitable and had detected a sigh of relief in the tired voice at the other end of the line. That sounded hopeful. Then she 'phoned Basil's sister and introduced herself, so sure of her success tomorrow that she booked a room at the hostel on the spot and arranged to move in first thing the next day. She met with the warmest of welcomes. Basil was an evident favourite with his sister, and his introduction seemed all-sufficient to open the door to Monica.

She hung up the receiver and went up to her room

to repack her suitcase, congratulating herself on her good fortune. She knew she could make a success of life; she knew Aunt Mollie was only being old-fashioned. Well, she supposed her aunt couldn't help it. Deliberately she banished her out of her thoughts. It did not do to dwell too long on Aunt Mollie, that was the trouble. She could easily dismiss the old, shallow relative as of no account, but the Aunt Mollie who had come home from Cobleigh Manor after her illness and had revolutionised the dull, dreary existence there was not so easily discredited. And yet, Monica found this new person very difficult to understand. Her own conversion while still at Glendorran had been real enough. A quiet, gentle experience, characterised mostly by a sense of relief and a new incentive to life which had brought her into line with the main body of her companions, whereas before she had set herself "agin the government" and across the trend of the life of the school. She had made strides ahead in her early Christian life in spite of her aunt's scorn, but when her aunt changed, too, and seemed suddenly to go on herself so much farther, Monica was already beginning her own spiritual landslide down from the sunny, happy heights into a dim valley of compromise that was dulling her testimony and having repercussions in the whole of her behaviour. Now she had grown to resent Aunt Mollie's progress, in the measure of her own backsliding.

So now, out of courtesy, she merely wrote a postcard, telling her aunt that she was in London, adding

the bold and presumptuous declaration that she had
a post and all was well. She promised to send details
when she had moved in. Stilling the twinges of conscience that told her she was giving neither adequate
nor accurate information, she stamped the card and
put it by her bag to post next morning. With that,
she undressed and went to bed, eagerly ready to face
the unknown experience of the days to come, satisfied that she was well able to champion her own cause
and guide her own footsteps into safe channels.

Certainly it did seem as if everything was falling
into place for her as by a magic touch. In that last
dreamy moment between sleep and only drowsiness
she roused herself to the possibilities of the new day,
utterly forgetful that she had anyone but herself to
thank for the rosy prospect she now faced.

Her neat little gold wristlet watch—a twenty-first
birthday gift from Uncle James—showed that it was
exactly ten o'clock when she ran up the steps of the
Home and pealed the bell. She had already dropped
in breezily to Basil's sister, left her case there and
promised to return in the early evening. She was
well pleased with all that she had seen both of
Basil's sister and of the hostel. Barbara Lorimer
was the right sort of contact for her to make, of
that she was convinced, and the attraction was
mutual.

Half an hour later, bare preliminaries were over.
Monica, once more clad in her pretty ivory and blue
overall with its ornate crest embroidered on it, was
back in harness. She thoroughly enjoyed the task of

bringing order out of the chaos that had followed the
sudden illness of her predecessor, leaving the busy
staff not only short-handed but ill-equipped to cope
with the specialised work of catering for a large
number economically. Monica surveyed her staff : the
cook she regarded a little cautiously. She was middle-
aged, and obviously considered herself a queen in
her own right in the kitchen. Oh, well, that suited
Monica. She had a cosy little room of her own with
a plate on the door bearing the one word "HOUSE-
KEEPER", and the younger members of the staff
seemed to expect to act as her messenger and go-
between, leaving her to plan and order and keep the
books, and generally administer stores and duties
alike. Monica felt a wave of satisfaction at the close
of that first day when Matron looked in to see how
she was getting on and was obviously both relieved
and impressed by her capabilities. The burden of responsibility for all the children and for this side of
the work, too, had fallen heavily on the one pair
of shoulders in the past two weeks.

In her work Monica was supremely happy. She
had deliberately chosen her career before leaving
school because she really loved the duties that would
be hers. Now as she took up these new responsibilities
the days slipped by in quick succession. Life seemed
suddenly to have gone bright and sunny. She was
needed and respected in the Home. She was made
welcome in the hostel, and was quickly popular with
the other young people, and Barbara had a way of
singling her out at the end of a day to spend an hour

in her own private sanctum, viewing television or listening to the wireless.

And yet, there was one cloud on the horizon. Miss Draper, the Matron, thankful to have Monica fill the vacancy that might need filling for several weeks if not months, had an intrinsic quality about her that made the girl uneasy. It was a quality that permeated the whole Home and gave character to it, and it was not lost on Monica. She had met it before in her Matron and her House-mistress and other members of the Glendorran staff. Here the young nurses had it too, that something that had marked out the merry bunch of students of her own year at College and whose company she had preferred so much that they had spent their holidays together at house-parties just because they knew the things of God mattered more than the things of the world. Monica often caught the soft humming of a hymn tune as she passed one or another of the staff, and heard snatches of conversation that told her quite plainly where their off-duty interests lay. For the first week Monica had been watchful. One word from Matron along that line and she would withdraw, ready to keep herself aloof and unapproachable, but so far no personal questions had been asked.

Punctually at five o'clock she peeled off her overall and tried to throw aside any more serious thoughts the day's contacts had created. Mostly she could manage well enough. There was nothing loud or rowdy about the hostel but there was always plenty to do, but invariably when she got into bed and put out

her light and was, at last, alone with her thoughts,
a growing sense of wistfulness was apt to creep in.
She tried to adjust herself to it. She compromised
with the best she knew and the second best she had
chosen : she started to say a short evening prayer
before slipping over to sleep, a sort of courtesy per-
formance—after all, as she reminded herself, she
was a Christian—and she tried to persuade herself
that such "belief" was all that was essential. If
some liked to go more deeply into matters she would
find no fault, but for her, just now, the barometer of
her life seemed to be set fair, and she was unwilling
to complicate matters by courting any storms.

The weeks passed uneventfully. It was a hot
summer, and each evening slipped by in lazy enjoy-
ment. And each evening she promised herself that
tomorrow she would write to Aunt Mollie. As the
beginning of August loomed in sight Basil spoke of
coming to visit them. At once Barbara began to make
plans. All her girls would be away. She and Monica
and Basil would take the week-end together at some
jolly place on the coast and have some real fun and
relaxation. She liked Monica, and was pleased that
Basil was attracted to her. Well, it shouldn't be her
fault if the friendship did not ripen satisfactorily.
She would see to it that they saw plenty of each other
under the most favourable conditions possible.

On the Friday evening Basil was there when Monica
got home from work. Barbara was the most perfect
chaperon-cum-hostess. All the other girls had left for
the week-end, and Mollie was invited to supper with

the brother and sister. Over the meal Barbara re-
told all the little family reminiscences of Basil's boy-
hood, and enlightened her brother on the discoveries
she had made of Monica in the past two months.
Then after supper, flatly refusing their assistance,
she turned them out into the garden to entertain
each other, promising to join them later with some
coffee.

Monica went to bed that night with her head full
of dreams, and with that delightful silvery "my
Monique" ringing in her ears. She felt again the
touch on her arm as Basil had opened the door for
her and warmed to the nice little attentions he had
paid both to her and to his sister as they sat together
through the evening. There was no doubt about it,
Basil was a very nice type.

The sunny week-end passed quickly. Indifferent
to all the crowds that seethed everywhere, the three
enjoyed every minute of the time. Bathing, playing,
picnicking: whatever they did was good fun. The
traffic on the roads was dense and, rather to Monica's
surprise, Barbara had kept the wheel firmly in her
own hands all the way there. Barbara, on the roads,
was the soul of carefulness, and Monica gathered
that she had a very low opinion of her brother's
standard of driving. By Monday night Basil was
determined to be thwarted no longer. Taking possession of the driver's seat, he and his sister had a heated
argument, much to Monica's embarrassment. Basil
won the day and started the car with a nonchalant,
couldn't-care-less manner, while Barbara sat at the

back with a hurt, don't-blame-me-if-anything-goes-wrong look in her eyes.

For a while all went well, although Basil was obviously showing off for Monica's benefit. Suddenly there was a terrific impact and a loud bang, and from that moment Monica lost trace of what was happening.

Some three hours later a very sobered, shocked brother and sister took themselves home by train. They were badly shaken but miraculously unhurt. Monica had fared far worse, and they had been obliged to leave her in hospital, still and unconscious, while they went back to reopen the hostel for the returning girls and tried to trace some relative to come and see the injured girl. Basil had vague recollections of her Uncle James, but they were vague, and the evening's disaster did not make it any easier for him to think clearly.

CHAPTER FIVE

BAD NEWS

WENDY and Christopher, standing side by side on the wide steps of the Manor House, had every reason to be feeling contented. They had just seen off the famous children's orthopædic specialist who was so interested in their experiment with the little patients. This man was, in fact, so keen that he had taken a day off to run down at his own request and see the place and the children for himself, accompanied by two surgeons who shared his concern. Enthusiastic over all that he saw, he had gone away, commending not only the generous host and hostess who were so using their home, but also Lindsey's capabilities and her competent helper. The children themselves had been such dears, contributing no little to the success of the day. Paul, blissfully indifferent to his twisted limbs, had hopped around, the cheerful host with the younger children, encouraging the newest arrivals not to be shy, and playing big brother to a little girl who eyed the great men very dubiously.

For a long while the two stood looking out over the expanse of lovely lawn and field and wooded slope that was their home.

"I spoke to Sir Nigel about the project for the pool, and he's all for it. He regards swimming as the finest exercise the children can have. We can go ahead at once now we have his approval."

Wendy looked up at her husband and smiled. "Granny really doesn't mind, does she?"

"No. She said she would miss the old landmark at first, but knowing what it will mean to the children, she's well satisfied to see it go."

The project for the pool was an idea that had been growing in their minds for quite a while. They planned to drain the water-lily pool, clean it and enlarge it, run in the water-heating system from the nearby conservatory and provide the children with a safe, warmed swimming-pool.

"Chris, darling, isn't it just wonderful what God has done for us?"

"It is, beloved."

To Christopher one of the greatest acts of the Lord's goodness had been the gift of Wendy to stand with him in all her love and loyalty, first to the Lord, and then to him and his responsibilities. How stalwart she had been to weather the storms that had more than once swept around them. It had been Wendy's courage and vision that had turned the disaster of Paul's crippling illness into the blessing it now was to themselves and to others.

There was an air of tranquillity about the hour. June and Lindsey were busy giving the children tea and telling them how good they had been. Marylin, Cook, and Veronica were indoors preparing the evening meal. In a few minutes Lennox would be back from the station, bringing with him the afternoon

letters. Every day Wendy waited expectantly for
a letter from Mollie giving news of the truant, and
any day now she was looking, too, for word from
her father and step-mother. They had sailed from
India, leaving the land they both loved for the last
time. Her father had been very ill, and the doctor
had strongly advised a return to the home country
and a quieter life in a more temperate climate. Andy
had promised to cable the date of their arrival, and
already the spare room was ready and waiting for
them.

"It would be nice to get some definite news of
Monica before Mother and Daddy come," Wendy
mused.

It was the second week in August now, and in
Mollie's last letter she sounded as if she was getting
pretty desperate. It really was too bad of Monica to
treat her aunt in that casual way.

Lennox swung the car into the drive and came to a
standstill at the foot of the steps. At the same moment
the 'phone bell rang in the house and Christopher
went indoors to take the call. Lennox handed over
the letters. Wendy flicked through them. She had
just recognised Mollie's handwriting when her husband rejoined her. Putting his hands gently round
her shoulders, he drew her into the house.

"Wendy, my darling, I'm sorry—but that was a
cable. Your father is ill again and wants you. They
were put off at Port Said and have been flown home.
Can you be ready in fifteen minutes and I'll drive
you to the hospital? I'll get Mother to come and see

to things; Lindsey and June will cope with the children splendidly. Come, darling—remember, there are no mistakes and no mistimings with our God.''

For one second Wendy was stunned and clung to her husband. Daddy ill enough to be flown home— and wanting her—now. She steadied herself. What a strength Christopher was, with his quiet faith and calm assurance.

"Yes, darling, I'll be ready, of course.''

She turned towards the stairs and went up to her room. She put down the letters and busied herself pushing the few essentials into a small bag. Snatching up her coat and gloves, she hurried away, leaving the day's mail unheeded on her table.

Two long hours of steady driving brought them to their destination. They had not talked much on the way. Christopher was driving as fast as he could, and gave all his attention to the job, but Wendy was silently pleading that they might be in time and that Daddy might yet be spared to come to them at Cobleigh and be cared for as she longed to care for him, and as she had so seldom had any opportunity to do in all her life.

At the main door of the hospital Christopher gave their names and the reason for their arrival. The porter 'phoned various departments and then ushered them into a restful waiting-room across the main hall. A tall, well-groomed figure stood with her back to them. As they came in, she turned, revealing as she did so a face worn with sleeplessness and anxiety.

"Wendy! Christopher! How wonderful of you to
come! And you can take her? Oh, you are dears!"

Mollie, completely unaware of the true situation,
fell on her two faithful friends joyfully. Suddenly she
saw the look of bewilderment and distress in Wendy's
eyes and stopped abruptly.

"You—you have come in answer to my letter?
You—you know about—Monica?"

She faltered.

The door opened behind them again.

"Lady Cardinal, will you step this way, please?"

Quickly Wendy's thoughts flashed into action.

"Mollie, no—a letter came, but I've not read it
yet. I'll explain later. Meanwhile, whatever you do,
don't go from here till we come back—promise?"

"Y—yes."

Reluctantly Mollie promised, sensing that her
friend had trouble of her own, but at a loss to fathom
the mystery. As the two left the waiting-room she sat
down in one of the long, low armchairs. There was
nothing to do now but wait, and wait as patiently as
possible. As she sat back Mollie realised, as she so
often did, how changed her life was. Not many years
ago such a wait would have cost her dearly in
cigarettes. Now, though she was anxious, anxious
for Monica, anxious for her friends, she was not restless. She had plenty to think about. The hospital folk
had been so kind to her, giving her lunch and tea, and
soon now she would be able to see Monica again.
How she hoped the Cardinals would be back before
then.

A whole hour dragged slowly by, Mollie glanced unseeingly at magazine after magazine, but not one word penetrated her busy brain. If Wendy couldn't take Monica, what then? She found herself nodding helplessly with sleep. She closed her eyes. She was tired out, first with her search for Monica and then all the travelling and talking and planning that had been her lot in trying to help the child now that she had found her.

Mollie woke with a start to find Christopher in the room and Wendy just coming in through the door with the unmistakable figure of Andy close beside her.

Quietly Christopher explained about Mr. Summers' illness, the unread letter, and the cable that had sent them hurrying here.

There were traces of tears on Wendy's face, but her voice was quiet as she took up the tale from her husband at its most difficult point.

"We were in time, Mollie; just in time. We saw Daddy, and he knew us just for a moment before he went."

Christopher sat down facing Mollie; Andy was in the other armchair, Wendy perched protectingly on the arm at her side. He leant forward listening to his wife's voice, his head cupped in his hands, his elbows bent on his knees. As Wendy paused he joined in, speaking more to himself than to anyone in particular.

"'And all the trumpets sounded for him on the other side'."

Instinctively Bunyan's great words satisfied them all, and Wendy looked across gratefully. How true that would be of Daddy. He had died as he had lived, quietly, yet with that gentle strength that had given purpose to all that he had done. He had gone to His Maker with clean hands and a pure heart, clothed in the robes of Christ's righteousness, un-afraid, untroubled.

Mollie did not know what to say or what to think. That these two whom she needed most should be here at this moment, and yet plunged into trouble more serious than her own left her unhappy and unsure of herself. Everything seemed to have gone wrong.

"I'm awfully sorry."

Mollie thought the words sounded absurdly tame and useless.

"And what is your news, Mollie?"

It was Wendy who asked, her arm still round her step-mother, a calmness about her that made Mollie marvel.

"Oh, it's a longish story. James got sent for by the son of a man he used to know in the old days. This boy knew Monica, she seems to have been staying at his sister's hostel, and the three of them were off on some spree on Bank Holiday and ended the day with a smash. They both got away with shock, but Monica got concussion and some broken bones. She can leave hospital now if she has any-where to go, and I'm fighting to get somewhere that will take her away from this boy's over-pressing attentions. She's not fit to travel to Glasgow, I can't take her to a hotel, and this boy and his sister are trying to get her to their place. I thought of you and Cobleigh at once when I found what a mix-up she had got herself into, but of course, now——"

Mollie broke off.

"But why not Cobleigh still? There's room, isn't there, Wendy? Isn't this what you keep the home for?"

It was Andy who spoke, and though her voice shook with recent emotion, her purpose in life was unshakable.

"Yes, but——"

Wendy was as amazed as the others.

"Well? You know your father, Wendy, as well as I do. Would he want the—the little we can do on earth for him now, to stand in the way of doing the Lord's work for one of His children?"

How like Andy, and how like her father! Wendy knew it was true and knew that Andy was right.

"But of course Monica must come, Mollie. Tell us more about the details. You know how big the Manor is—Mother will be with us, but that still leaves room. What does she need? A nurse? Or will you come? You'd be glad of this chance to be with her, wouldn't you?"

The door opened again, and the Matron's personal maid called Andy away and Christopher went with her. When they were alone Mollie found it easier to speak.

"Wendy, I feel so helpless. I don't know what to

say to comfort you. And then, here I am, loading you with fresh trouble. Are you sure we ought to come?"

"Quite sure, Mollie. It is what I would choose, though I admit I wouldn't have suggested it because of Mother, but as she feels like that, I'm sure it's right and best. It'll help her, I think, to feel there is still work to do now that so many hopes and plans will have to be set aside. She's not the sort to sit and fret, and yet she's bound to grieve, and I know she will be happier if the Lord gives her something else to go on doing right away. What are your plans? Are you staying here?"

Mollie named the hotel she was staying in, and when the others returned Christopher went off to book rooms for them all there. Over dinner that night Mollie brought them up to date with the small amount of news she had gleaned to fill in the gap of months since Monica had left the Glasgow home. She had met Basil and his sister, heard about the job and interviewed the Matron herself. It was good to know that Monica had at least worked well, and Mollie was sorry to have to know that Basil's stupidity had once again burdened the busy woman with the task of finding a housekeeper. Barbara she quite liked, but Basil did not at all find a place of softness in her heart.

CHAPTER SIX

A FAITHFUL FRIEND

M ONICA was not a good patient. Beyond an attack of measles while still at school she had never known a day's illness, and she did not take kindly to her present limitations. Her head ached if she tried to read, and a broken arm and leg hampered her activity. Her mood of frustrated independence did nothing to help. Mollie stayed on at the hotel while Wendy and Christopher took Andy home and went through the sad duties that had to be performed. She visited Monica as often as she was permitted, much to that maiden's disgust, as it now meant that she saw little of Basil and practically nothing of him alone.

Within a week word came that Cobleigh was ready for the guests, and Mollie thankfully made the necessary arrangements for the journey. To the children at the Manor the arrival at the house of an ambulance implied the coming of a new friend and playfellow, and they were disappointed to find the occupant was not being brought into their cheery dormitory and that she had not even a wave to spare to the little faces pressed against the glass watching the proceedings.

The next few days proved to be a testing time for

all the Cobleigh household, and Mollie was sometimes tempted to take Monica, sick though she was,
over her knee and spank her, at least metaphorically.
Wendy and Andy were taking their loss and disappointment with that silent triumph that had characterised Wendy at previous crises in her life, Christopher was busy on the estate, Granny Cardinal helping wherever she could find useful jobs that needed
doing. June and Lindsey always had their hands
full. Mollie felt hers was a difficult position, pacifying
Monica and encouraging her out of her despondency
and with the other hand keeping the determined Basil
in his place.

An hour that gave Mollie pleasure came between
tea and supper. Wendy and Andy insisted on taking
turns in the sick-room, one staying with the fretful
girl and the other taking Mollie off for a walk or a
drive. Tonight the two younger women went off together, leaving Andy reading aloud to Monica.

Basil had been to tea, and Monica had brightened
considerably during his visit. Not unnaturally, the
two friends fell to discussing him as soon as they were
alone together.

"It is a pity Basil is unsuitable for her," Mollie
sighed. She knew too well the folly of such a marriage, but it was quite another matter to be able to
persuade the young couple to see reason. "And the
trouble is he *has* nice ways and a good job. It's
awfully hard trying to get Monica to see that those
things are not enough."

"And she has so lost out spiritually herself that

they seem enough," Wendy added. "She is not
bothering with the standard that dismisses 'unequal
yoking' not as folly but as disobedience. Incident-
ally, will Basil keep his good job if he plays around
here much longer? Isn't it farming? And shouldn't
he be on the spot?"

"I would think so, but he says it's all right. He
works with his own family."

"May be they know him too well. Know he's not
reliable if his thoughts are somewhere else. He looks
a bit that sort to me. Spoilt son, do you think?"

"Could be."

A flight of wild fowl attracted their attention, and
they turned their thoughts to other channels.

Back at the Manor Andy had deliberately laid
aside the book after the first few pages. Monica was
not listening, anyway, but idly dreaming her own
day-dreams. The days were passing now, and none
of them at the Manor were at the root of Monica's
real trouble. Andy was kindness itself, but she never
made it easy for a wrongdoer to persist in her ways,
and she could be anything but easy going when she
came face to face with a situation that demanded
straight speaking, and therein lay a good deal of her
genuine kindness. Many a girl lived to be grateful
for the day that her Headmistress, or later, mis-
sionary's wife, had taken her aside and shown her
what she was and what she might be if she chose to
seek God's help to strive for it.

So now, without preliminaries, she came to the
point.

"When does Basil go back to work?"

"I don't know. There's no hurry."

"Why not?"

"His people said he needn't."

"That was kind, but not necessary. He can't do any good loafing around and spending good money."

"He's not loafing!"

"What is he doing?"

"He comes to see me when he's allowed in." Monica put unnecessary force into her words.

"Well?"

"He won't go back till I'm well enough to leave here. That's what he says, anyway."

There was a defiant note in her voice.

"Maybe he does, but we can't all live just as we like. You know that well enough."

"Why is everyone so horrid about Basil?"

Monica ignored Andy's last remark.

"No one is horrid, but you are being very foolish and unwise, and you know it. You are both far too young to be playing about like this."

"We are not playing!"

"I sincerely hope you are, Monica. I would be sorry to think you were seriously considering a life union with Basil."

"Well, I am. And why shouldn't I?"

Andy hesitated. Monica was such a child in some things and yet, for that very reason it was only honest to give her enough truth if she was to be expected to act in anything but a childish way.

"I will tell you why you should not, Monica. His

people are nice, certainly, but they are not the Lord's, neither is he, and he knows it. You are, even if you are not behaving like it just now—and that is something you will regret very soon. I'm afraid you must simply accept as fact that not only is it in direct disobedience to your Lord's request for you, as a Christian, to marry a non-Christian, but also that such a marriage simply does not work. Oh, I know, you think that in your case it would be different, but believe me, every young couple thinks that, and it never is so. God has very good reason for forbidding us to entangle ourselves—these lives which we profess to have handed over to Him and in which He has consented to give His own Spirit—with the life of one who owns no such standard and has not made the Lord Jesus Christ his Lord and Master. We who love you could never sit back and watch you do that, my dear. After all, Basil is your first taste of the attentive male, isn't he? And you must admit that you are hardly in a fit state to be judging such an important matter from a true Christian viewpoint, are you?''

Monica shrugged her shoulders.

"A lot of girls marry the first man they meet," she said pertly.

"But with all the other factors in this case, Monica, it makes a big difference. Tell me, what do you want out of marriage? What does it mean to you? I take it you are very happy in your career? You would not like to be classed with girls who marry to get away from the drudgery of their work?"

Monica was silent. Truth to tell, she never liked the hour when Aunt Mollie went off; it was bad enough with Wendy, but she would have far preferred to be left alone to dream of Basil than have Andy's company. She felt the challenge of Wendy's buoyancy and unperturbable faith, and knew a certain wistfulness in her heart at those times, but Andy was different. Monica had shrunk from meeting her as soon as she had heard of Mr. Summers' death, but an hour in her company had to be experienced to realise the influence it had upon one.

"Well?"

"Mrs. Summers." Monica spoke slowly, "I—I don't think I know. I don't know if I ought to ask this, not now—but, well, do you think you could tell me what it—it meant, to you?"

"Of course you may ask me, my dear, and I'll tell you gladly. Our marriage was based on mutual love and trust. You need those two ingredients. Not sloppy sentiment, but real love and utter trust. You need to want to put more in than you expect to get out of the marriage, you need to want to give before you want to get, but Monica my dear, the getting comes. When I married I was only aware of wanting to give, but I found the happiness of utter completeness in my husband. You need, too, to remember this: always, no matter what age, in every true man there lives something of the boy. Don't ever belittle it or try to crush it out. It is one of the dearest things about him. And in every girl there is something instinctive of a mother. That gives the woman that poise and balance she needs with men. The boy in Basil thinks it is the man. Rise to the real woman— the mother in you, and save him from his foolishness. Send him, gently, where he ought to be, back at his job.''

Monica lay and listened—the two Monicas rolled into one. One already mature enough to know that Andy was right, the other the child, hankering for Basil's attention as a child might grasp a sunbeam and mistake it for the sun. In her heart of hearts she knew which it was most worthwhile being, but in her present state of backsliding she had no power to resist the one and hold to the other, and so she only sighed and lay staring moodily out of the window when Andy left her a few minutes later and joined the others for dinner.

For the next few days Monica fluctuated between obvious attempts to be easier to nurse and more cheerful, and irritating sulks, but it was apparent to Andy that the girl had paid some heed to her homily and was spending several hours in more serious thought.

It was Friday evening—five days after their previous talk—before Andy was again sitting alone with the convalescent. Her arrival coincided with the departure of Basil, who had been permitted to come to tea, and Monica was in low spirits. The injured bones were well enough now to permit her moving about more easily, and Andy suggested they should go out into the cool evening and sit in the garden.

For a while Monica joined listlessly in the conversation, and then with abrupt directness told Andy what had happened.

"Mrs. Summers—I have told Basil and done what you said : sent him about his business. He's furious with me, but though I thought I'd feel perfectly miserable I don't. What bothers me is the other things you said. Talking to me you reminded me of the things we used to talk about at Glendorran and at Camp and—oh, I don't know, I feel as if I'd lost something. Mrs. Summers—help me !"

There was a note of urgent pleading in the girl's voice. Andy made her own silent, swift prayer for guidance as she punched up the cushions more comfortably behind Monica's head.

"Suppose you begin at the beginning, my dear, and tell me anything you'd like to," was the encouraging overture she gave.

"It's difficult to know where to start."

Monica was not looking at Andy, and her fingers were idly folding her skirt into pleats.

There was an awkward pause.

Andy tried another line of approach.

"I take it that what is really the heart of your trouble is that you have lost ground spiritually for some reason or another. When you want to be strong now and do what you know to be right you find yourself weak and ineffective. Would you say there were some chinks in your Christian armour, and so the enemy has got in, do you think?"

"I suppose so."

"Then all I can see for it is to go over that armour piece by piece and find out which is the bit and get it back firmly into place. What about the sword and the shield? Do you still read God's Word and trust both it and Him?"

Monica considered the question.

"I don't see how you can be sure about things like the Bible. Different people hold such differing views."

"I see. And at St. Adrian's you met different opinions from the convictions taught you at Glendorran?"

"Yes."

Andy said no more on that subject and passed on.

"What about the helmet of salvation—you haven't allowed doubts to enter your mind about being a Christian? You still believe that Christ died for you in order to deal with your inborn sin because there was no other remedy for it? He redeemed you, purchased you, from Satan's grip back to God?"

"Y—yes."

"Why the hesitation?"

"That seems so cut and dried. I mean we used to talk a lot about religion in the staff room at St. Adrian's. We had the most heated discussions and, well, crowds of really decent folk don't believe it need be as narrow and strict as all that. They would be horrified to talk about being 'born again'—and yet they are frightfully decent. I'd hate to say I was better than they are."

"I see."

Again Andy did not pursue that subject just then.

"You know, Monica, I think we could go bit by bit through all the armour and find that at St. Adrian's every bit had been pushed aside. Look, here's my pocket testament: let's turn up those verses. Here we are: Ephesians, chapter six, starting at verse ten. Will you read?"

"No, you, please."

Andy was aware that Monica meant business, and she knew how to read well. Slowly and thoughtfully she went over the passage:

"Finally, my brethren, be strong in the Lord, and in the power of His might. Put on the whole armour of God, that ye may be able to stand against the wiles of the devil. For we wrestle not against flesh and blood, but against principalities, against powers, against the rulers of the darkness of this world, against spiritual wickedness in high places. Wherefore take unto you the whole armour of God, that ye may be able to withstand in the evil day, and having done all, to stand. Stand therefore, having your loins girt about with truth, and having on the breastplate of righteousness; and your feet shod with the preparation of the gospel of peace; above all, taking the shield of faith, wherewith ye shall be able to quench all the fiery darts of the wicked. And take the helmet of salvation, and the sword of the Spirit, which is the word of God: praying always with all prayer and supplication in the Spirit . . ."

Then, laying the book open on her knee, she took the girl's slim-fingered hand in her own friendly grasp.

"Look, Monica, you left Glendorran and college strong and eager—but perhaps you were 'strong in Monica' and not 'strong in the Lord'. And you see, our first instruction is to don the whole armour and take our firm stand, and then go on to withstand. We must take that first initial stand, fully equipped, if we are to withstand. St. Adrian's was a bit different from school and college, wasn't it? You thought you'd better feel your way and be a little cautious. You waited to see how the land lay before you were too definite as a Christian, isn't that so?"

Monica studied the strong hand, tanned with India's sun, and felt miserable. How exactly that described her arrival at St. Adrian's! She had thought herself "diplomatic", but Andy's suggestion of caution and indefiniteness was a much truer description.

"And so," Andy went on again, "you ran into difficulties. You cannot withstand a foe while you are still fumbling around to get into your armour—especially when some of it is already mislaid or rusty. You left it too late. He took advantage of that and attacked while you were ill-prepared. Let's look at the pieces again and see how perfectly they meet our every need. 'Loins girt with truth'—loins is another word for thighs, isn't it? And your thighs really make the whole of your body go in the direction your legs take it. Loins, then, concern our walk.

You can move your toes and knees and legs and not walk one inch. God says He gives you truth to gird around your loins. What does that mean? Surely that you must walk through life as what you are— a born-again Christian. Be true to Him. Don't hide your real life under a cloak of being 'like the rest', 'easy-going', and all that sort of thing. Be what you are at heart. And then, 'the breastplate of righteousness'—your feelings and affections governed by integrity and your love placed where it belongs—first and foremost for the Lord. In Basil you let your emotions carry you away because he was nice and attentive and made a fuss of you. Had your heart been set on love for the Lord that temptation would not have held so much attraction for you.

"And what about your shoes? Did you carry the gospel to St. Adrian's? Ill-shod feet only make us stumble when the road gets rough, but if we travel as His ambassadors the road doesn't hurt us, our witness for Him keeps our feet, and He travels the road with us. Your shield of faith was very dull and rusty. Regular use keeps it bright, nothing else. Only when we keep to solid convictions are we safe from dents in that piece of armour. Job made use of the shield—'I KNOW that my Redeemer liveth', so did Paul—'I KNOW Whom I have believed'. And we come into a long line of faithful victorious warriors when we cling to our shield. And the world needs that confidence—it is a very restless, uncertain, unhappy world, Monica. And then the helmet. I've always liked this bit. It covers the head, and so many of our troubles start with drifting thoughts, entertained doubts and fears, foolish wisdoms of men who would persuade us that they can plan a better way of salvation for us than the one our loving Creator has designed at great cost to Himself.

"But, what about your Bible reading and prayer?"

Monica nodded dully; it all seemed so stupid now.

"Yes, I guessed so. To skip that is such a pitfall, and so often young Christians get a bit *blasé*—the day's portion is a more familiar passage, so we think we know it all and miss for a day or two—oh, I know it, and it is *such* a danger. Monica, never again slip into the way of missing your reading and prayer and promising yourself you'll catch up later on, it just does not work. You would never dream of going without your meals, and reckoning on a bumper feast at the end of the week. You'd be too flabby by then to take the food—and that is exactly the same. Starve yourself of spiritual nourishment and you lose the appetite for it."

Monica was now the picture of despair. Andy gave her hand a gentle pat.

"Now, come along, there's no need to stay in your Slough of Despond once you recognise where you've got to. Come up out of it. You don't want to follow the modern trend of those who cover up their hearts' dissatisfaction with a show of cheap phraseology. I know you really want to be a single-hearted follower of Jesus Christ, now don't you?"

c

"Oh, Mrs. Summers, I *do,* truly I do. I've been miserable for months. I knew things were going wrong, but I only half wanted to get them right. The popular way seemed so much more comfortable. I sometimes wish I'd never gone to St. Adrian's. It would have been so much easier at a school like Glendorran."

"Yes, dear, it would have been easier, and if God dealt with us as we deal with hothouse plants you might well have gone to such a school. But you see, both at school and at college there were others there before you, and all you had to do was join forces with them. At St. Adrian's you had to stand alone. It is one thing to be staunch when we have props all around us, and quite another to remain standing when the props are removed. That proves if the life is from within or from without. God in His wisdom keeps us in the hothouse for just a while and then hardens us off and finally puts us out to weather the storms, sustained by life within. Don't look so downcast. This experience has taught you to dig your roots in deeper—deeper into His Word. And one thing that Word says is this: 'When He hath tried me I shall come forth as gold.' You know how gold is heated and heated to remove all the dross, until only the pure gold is left? Don't be afraid of the heat, Monica, He takes care of that Himself, but remember every testing time is designed to rid us of a bit more dross and leave behind a bit more purer gold."

The sun was sinking down behind the hills and

casting long, grotesque shadows over the lawn. Far away a sheep bleated. Monica lay back in her chair silent but no longer sullen. Without a word, Andy gently withdrew her hand and slipped away indoors to get Monica's cardigan and her own, meanwhile leaving the girl alone with her new and happier thoughts.

CHAPTER SEVEN

THE OPENING OF THE SWIMMING-POOL

SEPTEMBER 9th was as perfect as a mid-summer day. At Cobleigh Manor excitement was rising as rapidly as the mercury in the thermometer in the hall. This was the great day—the day of the official opening of the new swimming-pool, and because the children had all too few treats and outings, Christopher and Wendy had planned to make a real celebration of the event, complete with the children's parents and the many interested friends from the estate and the village. There was to be a display by the children, sports for the visiting children, and a tea with ices.

Wendy had thought it would be nice if Granny Cardinal would perform the simple little ceremony of cutting the "chain" of beautiful gold ribbon that was to be hung across the pool to signify this opening, but she was horrified at the idea, loudly disclaiming any virtue as a celebrity such as this event demanded. There was no moving her, but she went to work quietly on her own, and while the others were still keeping the matter open in the hope of persuading her at the last minute, she prevailed upon none less than Sir Nigel Gilmour, the children's own great specialist.

Every nook and cranny was full of bustle and

activity. Lindsey and June had their hands more than full, and were glad to welcome a volunteer helper in Monica. Since her second talk with Andy, Monica had taken strides forward, and was rapidly recovering both her bright witness as a Christian and her physical health and strength.

Christopher was Master of Ceremonies, and was thoroughly enjoying himself; there were potatoes and spoons and large handkerchiefs to collect for the visitors' races. A stack of nicely warmed towels for the swimming-bath, a megaphone, a hand-bell, and all the rest of the paraphernalia for such a day.

Mollie was helping Granny Cardinal with the teas and refreshments, aided by all the Manor and Dower House staff, who looked upon this day as their day, just as they regarded the little patients as their special care whenever they could be of any service to them. "Our" children were well known all over the village.

Paul and wee Elspeth were handed over to Nannie Gorson, and nothing pleased the three of them better than to be together. That left Wendy free to meet the guests and mingle among them.

Punctually at half-past two after a hectic half-hour of arriving motor cars and taxis, hand-shaking and chattering, a long, slim, blue car pulled into the drive and drew up at the main entrance to the Manor House. A hush of eager expectancy stilled the noisy tongues, and everyone craned forward for a glimpse of the guests of honour. The chauffeur stepped out smartly and opened the doors; Sir Nigel got out and turned to help Lady Gilmour. A moment later another car drew up behind, and four more interested doctors joined the party. Christopher and Wendy greeted their guests together and then led the way to the raised platform that had been erected the day before at the head of the pool. Everyone clapped their arrival, and Nannie gave Elspeth a gentle little push forward. The child hesitated. Instantly Paul struggled to his feet and took her hand, and together the pair went up to the platform.

Elspeth still stared up at the smiling faces, her free hand clutching a bouquet of red and gold rosebuds firmly.

"Go on, Puff," Paul used his own baby name for his little sister. "Give the lady the flowers."

Suddenly Elspeth forgot her shyness and, shaking herself free of her big brother, she held up the flowers and her small round face, waiting for the kiss that most people gave her when she gave them flowers. Lady Gilmour knew just what was expected of her and bent to kiss the soft pink cheek. But Elspeth had forgotten Paul and Nannie Gorson in her delight at this kind lady and promptly climbed up and sat on her knee, to Lady Gilmour's great joy and everyone's amusement.

"Puff shouldn't have done that," Paul remarked solemnly as he took his place beside Nannie, but Nannie only smiled down at him and reassured him that his little sister had not really disgraced the family.

Sir Nigel wasted no time on unnecessary speeches

and empty words. He knew that Christopher and Wendy had wanted to do this thing and would not thank him for making a fuss of them in public, though he did use the time to tell the parents what a boon the swimming-pool was going to be to their needy children. He knew, too, all about the excited little people who were eager to get their bit of the display safely over, so after only the shortest possible speech he took up the large pair of scissors that lay on the table and stepped forward and slowly and carefully cut through the beautiful ribbon the children had made into links themselves specially for the occasion.

That was the signal for the fun to begin. The two oldest boys, Johnny and Rex, were helped down into the clear water, and for several minutes duck-dived to the bottom, bringing up gaily coloured rings and blocks to the delight of the onlookers. Then three younger children went in, swam for a little and then turned neatly on to their backs and floated calmly to the side, gently washed there by June, who was in the water with them and was now making waves big enough to carry them to the bank and to Lindsey's strong arms to help them out.

Finally, as far as the children were concerned, two small grinning boys, one of them Paul, were lowered into the water, safely secured by a belt and a rope, one in Lindsey's care, and the other in Christopher's . With much excitement and much splashing and fun the pair "swam" the length of the bath with elaborate and energetic breast strokes.

Each event was given a great round of applause, and the children went off to be dried and dressed, well pleased with their efforts. While this was taking place, June, who had been something of a swimming champion at Glendorran, entertained the guests with a display of diving and very beautiful swimming.

As she came up out of the water for the last time Christopher rang his hand-bell and announced through his megaphone that tea was being served on the lawn, to be followed in half an hour by sports in the big field for the visiting children.

It was during the tea interval that Monica came into her own. Wendy, Christopher, Andy: all were busy talking to parents and making the best use possible of the time afforded them in this way to get to know and help the parents all they could. Monica was helping a small child with her ice-cream. The specialist and his friends were wandering at will talking to the children, to Lindsey, and to any parent who wanted to speak with them. Everywhere was an atmosphere of friendliness. Lady Gilmour, passing Monica and the child, noticed Monica's sling and bound-up foot. She stopped until the child was finished.

"Are you a patient, too?" she asked Monica, as the child ran off.

"Not really, not polio. I had an accident; my aunt knew Lady Cardinal, and they've been awfully good having me here. My home's in Scotland, and it was too far for me to travel."

Lady Gilmour was watching the happy young

face. She noted the light in her eye and the natural-
ness of her manner. She sighed. All these people here
seemed to have that quality about them that reminded her strangely of her own childhood and
home.

"Sir Christopher and Lady Cardinal are good,
aren't they? Very good." She paused half-wistfully.

"They are." Monica was not sure what she was
meant to say. She knew her friends would be the
last people to want to be called "good", but she
knew what Lady Gilmour meant.

They both stood silent for a minute, both watching Wendy, deep in conversation with an anxious
mother.

"What is your name, my dear?"

"Monica. Monica O'Riley."

"Well, Monica, can you explain this place. What
makes it the happy place it is? My husband just
raves about it for the children, and when he's been
down here he seems to come home—well, very gentle
and quiet. He's always a dear, don't mistake me,
but he seems at his best when he's been here, as if
something had influenced him for good."

Monica hesitated. Not many days ago she would
literally have had nothing to say, but then, no one
would have been likely to ask her such a question.
Now she looked up happily.

"I think the explanation of this place is just that
Sir Christopher and Lady Cardinal really believe
God in a very simple but positive way and live, day
by day, putting that faith into practice. Those of us

who come under their influence come to something more than just a happy family and a happy home. At least, I know I've met a definite challenge myself. I was not living up to the best I knew when I came here not so very long ago, but they make nothing half-hearted seem worthwhile."

The ringing of Christopher's hand-bell to announce the children's sports put a stop to any further conversation, and the two separated.

Over in the big field the spectators were taking their places on long wooden benches down each side, and the children were clamouring to enter for the different races. Soon the cheering and the shouting started. Potato "eggs" tumbled out of wobbling spoons, while the one or two successful champions struggled on, small tongues peeping round the corners of small mouths as the concentration grew greater. Partners teamed up to have their feet tied together for a three-legged race, human wheel-barrows lined the starting tape, teams got together for relays, and so the fun went on until everyone was worn out with laughing and clapping and shouting.

At last the sun began to dip and the crowds began to move towards the gate, nodding to the waving children and to Wendy and Christopher as they passed. There was no doubt about it, the day had been a great success and everyone was well satisfied.

"You're doing a fine job of work, Cardinal." Sir Nigel had one last word with his host as they were preparing to leave.

The car pulled away from the house. The children

were being put to bed. The family were alone at last. Out on the quiet terrace they exchanged news of one and another. What Mr. and Mrs. Wilson had said. What the doctors had thought of the whole project. What the village folk had made of the day. Shyly Monica added her contribution, telling of her meeting with Lady Gilmour. Over her head Wendy and Andy exchanged glances full of meaning. This was the real Monica. Satisfied that, once again, both in Monica and in Lady Gilmour, seed had been sown that might yet bear much fruit, they went indoors together to get ready for dinner.

CHAPTER EIGHT

A SECOND CHANCE

As Monica settled herself in the corner seat of the railway carriage she heaved a sigh of relief. That had been a near thing. She was due at the hospital that day for a final check-up and wanted desperately to go on her own—she had designs for the rest of the day, but all the Cobleigh family seemed to have conspired together with kind suggestions for accompanying her. It was only now, as the train really pulled out of the station, that she could be certain that she had succeeded, very politely, in shaking them all off without rousing their suspicions or hurting their feelings.

The visit to the hospital came up to her expectations. Managing to be well on time, she was seen first and speedily dismissed. That was exactly what she had hoped for. Now, if she could catch a fast train to town, she could carry out the rest of her plan and still get the afternoon train back to Cobleigh. That would connect with the local train which she would be expected to catch after the hospital visit.

All went well. With bare seconds to spare she caught the London train, and within an hour was walking into the entrance of the Station Hotel. Lunch was a minor detail. She had snatched some biscuits and chocolates as she hurried past the confectionary kiosk at the station and had no time to wait for the threepence change. She had one goal in view, and was determined nothing should stand in her way. So far everything was working out almost miraculously. As she stood in the hotel vestibule waiting to give her name at the desk she thought how right Mrs. Summers was when she said that the Christian life was full of adventure if one learned to trust God and follow His leading. If anyone had told her a month ago what she would be doing today she would have laughed at them and thought the very idea wholly fantastic.

She stepped forward as her turn came and gave her name at the desk. She waited hopefully, breathlessly. Yes, she was expected. The girl in the desk directed her to the lounge. At that moment the lounge door swung open and there they were, face to face, Miss O'Riley the ill-mannered, immature matron, and "Johnny", the decent head of St. Adrian's, who had been sorry to have to see her go on her wilful way unchecked.

When Andy had spoken so plainly to Monica the girl had felt a longing to put matters right at St. Adrian's. She knew only too well that "Johnny" had not been to blame, not for one bit of the trouble. She almost wished she could go back and start again. But she knew that was only wishful thinking. Life wasn't like that. One couldn't make a mess of some opportunity and then get the chance all over again and do better. One had to learn by one's mistakes and take care not to repeat them—that was the best one could hope for. She tried to put the affair out of her mind. It wasn't so easy. For one thing she had been abominably rude to "Johnny", and at least she ought to write and apologise to him. That wasn't so easy either, but eventually, unknown to anyone at Cobleigh, it was done and the letter posted. After that Monica felt better and had settled to all the fun of the Swimming-Pool Opening. With the whole affair out of her mind, she had been surprised to see a letter at her place one morning written in "Johnny's" scholarly hand and with the familiar post-mark. She opened it with rather shaky fingers. Would he accept her apology? Would he be nice? Or would he take the opportunity to rub in some of his very apt home truths a little harder? Well, she couldn't blame him if he did.

That letter was one of the kindest Monica had ever received. He not only accepted her apology but he also sympathised over her unfortunate accident. And then he added a suggestion. If she was not fixed up with a permanent job, would she care to consider returning to St. Adrian's in the autumn? He would be in town in the middle of September, and would be happy to give her an interview when they could discuss the whole position.

Again Monica had said nothing to the family. Not that she wanted to hide this opportunity from them, but because it could so easily seem to be the right way to go. If she said nothing about it, and yet the way opened for her to get to an interview with "Johnny" by herself, without recourse to any sub-

terfuge or untrue evasion, well, she would take that
to mean that at least the interview was being planned
for her by the Lord. It would be time enough after
that to share any possible return to St. Adrian's
with the family.

And now, here she was, face to face with the Head-
master, and very conscious that not only had God
guided her steps in spite of all her foolish waywardness, but also that she wanted Him to have the leading now. With a little whispered prayer in her heart
that she might make no mistake, she greeted Mr.
Johnson with a shyness that was born of the unhappy recollection of their last meeting.

"Here we are, then, Miss O'Riley! How nice to
see you—and no slings and splints and crutches,
that's splendid!"

Talking cheerfully to put the girl at her ease,
"Johnny" led the way back into the Lounge and
ordered coffee from a waiter as he passed.

Gratefully Monica followed and sat down in the
comfortable armchair that he pulled forward for her,
in the deep recess beside the window. The waiter
brought the coffee and a plate of sandwiches, and the
two helped themselves while the man did the talking. Monica sat and listened. For the first time in her
young life she was seeing things in a new way, seeing
with a clearer, more mature perception. "Johnny",
for her own good, was being very frank with her.
He meant business, and if she meant business with
him this time, all would be well. And the new Monica,
the Monica who had had the sense to be ashamed of

herself and her foolish ways, had the grace to listen to his words of wisdom.

Within an hour the interview was over. Monica was again engaged as a junior matron to the smallest boys' dormitory at St. Adrian's, and the prospect thrilled her.

As she journeyed home she thought how she would break her news to the others. They would all be pleased, she was sure of that; and they would all forgive her for her secrecy over the interview, she was sure of that, too. What a nice family they were! Of course, she could never do anything but regret her accident and the months she had wasted first in stupid bumptiousness, thinking herself far cleverer than her aunt and the jolly old crowd at Glendorran, and then fooling around with Basil and its unhappy result, but for all that, since she had been backsliding, she could never be anything but grateful that she had gone to Cobleigh and met with such patience and kindness there. As the train pulled in to Cobleigh Station she felt the thrill of being home and of having brought with her something worth sharing with the others.

As she had expected, her announcement was greeted with both surprise and pleasure, and even Aunt Mollie did not rebuke her for not having taken her into her confidence. But later that evening, alone for a few minutes before dinner with Andy, Monica revealed the very heart of her interview with Mr. Johnson.

"Mrs. Summers, when he said that because my

school and college references spoke of me as a Christian he had engaged me in the first place, I felt dreadful. He opened up quite a bit—talking almost as if I wasn't there—about ideals he'd had as a boy, but which he'd lost somewhere along the line at college and in later life. Now he seems to know that most of the staff are quite vague in their faith and haven't got anything solid to give the children, and yet he wants them, specially the youngest ones, to get it in their out-of-school time, as they should be doing at home. So he wants to get Christian matrons. That's why he appointed me. I was to be a sort of test, and if it worked he'd get others. He's been awfully decent; he admits it was tough to be the only one. He's got another in mind for the youngest girls —she's from a keen home, and her people are missionaries. He thinks we'd be able to help each other. Oh, Mrs. Summers, when Johnny was speaking I couldn't help seeing how near I'd come to disaster. Not only for myself, but also for St. Adrian's and for those youngsters. If Johnny hadn't been willing to try again—if he'd judged all keen Christians by me —it would have spoilt everything.''

"Monica, my dear, I am glad. This sort of thing doesn't often happen, as you have recognised. But since it has happened for you, I do not think you will go into this new experience lightly.''

"Pray often for me, will you? You've been such a dear helping me to find my way back to Him. In some ways it won't be any easier in the staff room than it was before, but, though I don't want to be stand-offish, I don't need to be there nearly as much as I used to be. I used to go for the fun of a good argument.''

"Never court danger, Monica. If you meet it, stand up to it with all your armour on and do not be afraid. But don't go looking for it. From what you say of your job you won't really have very much spare time for chattering with staff."

"I certainly shall not. Half the time before I sneaked from other duties, persuading myself that we matrons were over-worked just because we had different hours from the school staff. I shall see quite enough of them to be able to meet any who really seriously want any help—and only this morning in my reading I got the dig I needed from Titus."

"Which bit was that?" Andy looked amused.

"Avoid foolish questions! And how foolish they are! When I think of the hours that we wasted discussing and discussing, and of course we never arrived at any conclusion."

"You wouldn't!"

Monica joined in the laugh, and then the two said good night.

"When does the term start, Monica?" Wendy asked next morning.

"Next week as ever is! Johnny has given me till after that first week-end if I need it, but I'd like to be in at the start if possible."

"So you'll be getting busy and leaving us?"

"Yes," Mollie took up the tale. "Monica and I were talking about it last night. She wants to call in

at Barbara's for her things and just run in and see
the Matron of that place, so I suggest we take a day
in town together and do any shopping she needs and
travel up to Glasgow by the night train—say on
Thursday. That would give us a long week-end at
home before she needs to leave again on Wednesday
for school.''

"I see. That sounds a good plan, only this is
Tuesday, so we must make the most of these two
days, Monica. You haven't really begun to see the
sights around Cobleigh. As Paul would say, you
haven't been a real visitor until you've done the
round of our lovely land-marks and picnicked on the
top of the hills. We'll have to see if it's a nice day tomorrow.''

It was, and the family packed itself into the two
cars and set off for the day to visit the castle, the old
market town, the river, and to climb the winding
path up the hill and picnic there above the wide
panorama of valley and plain, hamlet, and town,
and to watch the sun ride over the top of the hills
and slip majestically away behind them in a blaze of
colour.

CHAPTER NINE

A NEW IDEA

THE departure of Monica and Mollie from Cobleigh Manor and the first nip of early autumn coincided, and instinctively Wendy and her stepmother turned their thoughts towards the winter that lay ahead. Much as they delighted in having the Manor used to help one and another, they were far from bored in each other's company, and now that their guests were gone the two spent long days together. Both were having to adjust in every way to the gap left by the home-call of Mr. Summers, and Wendy had the disappointment of never really having lived at home with her father. Even so, she knew she could not measure that in the least against the sense of loss that was Andy's. Christopher, too, had his own disappointment. He had looked forward eagerly to the friendship and the wisdom of his father-in-law, and had often, recently, put off decisions, thinking to share the matter first with the older man before passing his own judgment on it. But the little family found itself drawn closer together in its mutual loss, and the days that passed in the slow golden procession of autumn were happy days indeed.

It was on a chill October evening that Christopher's mother came in to see them. She was often in and out, especially with the children, but she seldom joined them in the evenings now that the night air was cold, and besides, one of her most rigid, self-imposed stipulations to their relationship was that she came into their evenings only by invitation. Evenings, she said—at least the few that Wendy and Christopher managed to get at home alone together —were very much their own, and she refused to break in on them. This was different. As soon as they saw her the young people knew she had something of importance that had brought her. Sure enough, she had.

"I've had a letter," she began when they had drawn another big chair up to the cheery fireside for her. She fumbled in her bag. "Here it is. It's from your Aunt Margery, Christopher, and a pathetic bit of a letter it is, too. She's never settled down to make anything of life since your Uncle John died, and now she says that she's in her bed more than she's out of it and only the servants to see her; and half the time they don't even answer her bell until she has rung for a third time. It's the great old house, you know. You can't wonder servants won't stay. I've lost count of how many changes she's had, and that means they just go there because it's easy money."

Christopher had taken the offered letter and was reading it, his kind eyes troubled. He had only the dimmest recollection of Uncle John and Aunt Margery—he believed he used to meet them at some of the larger family social functions, and had never felt drawn to this very glittering aunt and pompous uncle. But now—it was different now. Pomp and glitter were small comfort when one was old and ill and helpless, dependent upon unscrupulous staff and diminishing means. He wondered what he could do. He glanced at Wendy. This wasn't just the purpose they had always in mind for Cobleigh, especially now that the children's work was developing. They had, in fact, quite other thoughts. Thoughts of turning over the great lounge to accommodate more children, and dividing their own enormous dining-room into two, lounge and dining-room. It was big enough. But of course, Aunt Margery's was a very real need. He hesitated. They had given the Manor to God, and they could trust Him to show how they were to use it. He would not ask two things of them at once. Perhaps their plan was all wrong.

"May I show Wendy?"

He held the letter out to his mother.

"But of course."

Wendy read it in silence and then looked at her husband, reading in his face his willingness to help.

"Could we help her here do you think, Granny?" she asked, but Lady Cardinal shook her head firmly.

"No, my dears; I know you would, but I'm sure that's not the right way. No, Margery needs me. She needs a bit of mothering, just as I used to mother her when we were small, even though she is two years my senior. And those servants—you wait till I get there! I'll make them sit up and do their work properly. Leaving the poor soul with her bell un-answered indeed! No, I'm going to pack up and go

to her. That's my place, and I've come to my senses
in time, by God's grace and your goodness to me;
I can yet be of some use to one of my own. You can
do what you like with the Dower House, Christopher.
I doubt if I'll need it again by the time I've seen
Margery through, and I mean to stick to her as long
as she's here to need me.''

There was a significant pause as she finished. Each
was busy with the thoughts this news had aroused.
The old Lady Cardinal had indeed given place to the
new.

Wendy persuaded her mother-in-law to stay with
them for their evening cup of tea, and over that they
talked about the practical ways and means of such
a momentous decision. Wendy insisted that Lady
Cardinal should stay with them the last few days
while all her things were being sent off, a suggestion
which was gratefully accepted. Christopher saw his
mother home later that night, and the two walked in
silence. When they reached the Dower House mother
and son went in together.

"Sit down, Christopher. I won't keep you, but
just this I want to tell you. Away back from that
first day when you tried to tell me of your discovery
of Jesus Christ in the beginning of your army training I knew perfectly well what you meant, and I mis-
understood you intentionally. I had seen a little of
what the life of Christ within a human life can do.
Things have to change. I hated change. Things have
to be cleaned up, lives in which He has room to dwell
cannot be careless, happy-go-lucky—though only

now do I know how carefree they truly are, but that
is different. I did not want a disciplined life. I did
not want to be made to think about the future. Then
I saw things happening. You, Wendy, Lindsey, your
father, Mrs. Harris, even our own staff. I resented
it all, but I was watching. One thing which held me
back was that I could see we could not take and
enjoy this life, hugging it to ourselves. We had to
give out what we received. I used that as a blind
excuse to stay as I was. My family—you and Wendy
—had it for yourself; Cobleigh was getting it if they
wanted it. My circle wouldn't accept, they would
only drop off altogether. It was easy to make myself
believe I had left it too late and might as well face
that fact and go on as I was going. But—well, you
know the rest. The Lord used your beloved little
Paul, and I'll never cease to be thankful. And now,
at last He has given me someone who needs me. I
go to your Aunt Margery not only to care for her
body but also to help her find her Saviour. Christopher, it won't be easy, but isn't it wonderful to think
that the Lord can give even an old woman like me
something to do—some little share in His work. I
couldn't not go now, whatever the cost.''

Christopher went home very thoughtfully to share
this latest news of his mother with his wife. As the
two lay awake quietly talking, a new plan began to
form in Christopher's mind. With his mother's removal he was free to do as he would with the Dower
House, and suddenly he saw just how very useful it
was going to be. Wendy was obviously asleep, so he

resisted the temptation to leap up and make his plans at once, but after breakfast next morning he waylaid Wendy as she came out of the nursery, and the two were shut in his den for a long time before he set off on his usual morning round of the estate.

After Christopher had left the house Wendy went in search of Andy, her eyes shining as she tried to grasp the full force of her husband's suggestion. Andy was in the hall, just in from the garden, a bunch of glorious gold and red chrysanthemums in her hands.

"Aren't they gorgeous, Wendy?"

Wendy linked arms with her step-mother, admired the lovely flowers and piloted her into the den she had so recently left.

"Christopher was late this morning and wouldn't wait for coffee. We'll take ours here while I tell you the most amazing news."

Wendy rang the bell, and the two settled companionably on the small easy couch that stood pulled invitingly up towards the fireplace. A small electric heater glowed cheerily in the hearth, though the lattice windows stood open to catch any sun that might come in, and the room was full of the sweet scent of a nearby bonfire.

"Well, what's the excitement?"

Andy helped herself to sugar as the two were left alone after the arrival of Veronica and the coffee.

"You heard Granny's proposal last night? Well, quite suddenly Christopher has seen what this could mean for the children. He suggests that we move into the Dower House ourselves—it's more than big enough even to have good staff and a guest room—Granny hasn't been using half the rooms really. Then, if Sir Nigel agrees, the Manor can be used entirely for children, except this den. I think Christopher would keep that as his own sanctum for estate work, and seeing people, and studying."

"Wendy, how wonderful!"

At once Andy was wholeheartedly interested, caught up in all the possibilities.

"I've seen one snag."

Wendy laughed ruefully. She hated having to put a practical objection in the way of any of her husband's schemes, because usually they were so thoroughly sound and well worked out beforehand.

"What's that?"

"We can live a good deal more economically ourselves at the Dower House, and of course we can give the Manor over to Sir Nigel as a sort of Trust, if he cares to have it—and Christopher is pretty sure he'll jump at it—but we can't endow it. I think it all hangs on seeing what Sir Nigel has to say about it."

"The parents, or some scheme, I suppose, pay for the children?"

"Oh, yes, but it would mean more staff and more equipment, and the house takes a good bit to run. We could help, but it would not be anything like enough."

The two sat on, weighing the pros and cons until

Paul came in search of his mother, Elspeth close at his heels.

Three days later Sir Nigel dined with them and listened eagerly to the proposal. Every detail seemed only to make him more keen, and he and Christopher sat in the den, paper and pencil in hand, sketching plans, discussing the hundred and one aspects of such an opportunity. The financial side Sir Nigel found no trouble. True, he could not do more himself than give his services, as he so willing did and would continue to do, however big the "family" grew to be, but he was quite certain he knew people whose hearts and purses could be touched to meet such a need as this.

Well pleased with the venture and quietly outspoken as to their indebtedness to the Cardinals, the great man went away, and at once the wheels began to turn.

The Dower House needed some repairs and alterations, and Lady Cardinal planned to join her sister at the end of November. With all that needed to be done and arranged, the date for handing over the Manor and their own removal to the Dower House was put off until the beginning of January. Meanwhile Christmas lay between them and that removal. With one accord the two young people, aided and abetted by Andy, began to make plans for a full house over the holiday. All the children would be going to their parents, though some would return to be joined by new-comers. For those few days, perhaps stretched to a week, the house should be filled with as many friends as possible : Jim and Mollie, Lindsey and her mother, June and the rest of the old Dormitory crowd, Monica, perhaps Miss Bridger and Miss Carpenter could be persuaded into coming. So the list grew, and the shortening days, the fogs and the rain, and the winds that howled at night passed almost unheeded as every member of the family found the days busier than ever before if all was to be ready in time. Paul and Elspeth lived in a world of magic. Christmas was a joy and a delight in itself, but this year, surrounded as it was with builders and painters at Granny's house, packing-cases and trunks and wonderful treasures being turned out of long-forgotten hidey-holes, the promise of a house full of aunties and uncles, and the interesting smells of Christmas cooking, the two children found life very exciting.

CHAPTER TEN

ST. ADRIAN'S

"READY, Monica?"
    "Shan't be a tick!"
The voice was the voice of Pearl Adams, the senior
matron in charge of St. Adrian's sick bay, and
Monica snatched up the letters she had been writing
and hurried out of her room to join her new friend.
It was half-term, and there were no children with
colds or temperatures or twisted ankles to keep either
of them in, and the two had long planned to spend
this Saturday together if they could.

"What's Winsome doing?" Pearl asked, as they
left the school behind them and walked to the bus
stop.

"Don't ask me! Tidying her room, washing, writing letters—goodness knows what else. I really think
she feels its quite iniquitous to take a day off and
thoroughly enjoy yourself!"

"Poor kid! You know, Monica, I sometimes
wonder if we understand Winsome. I wonder if she
ever has, as you say, 'taken a day off and enjoyed
herself'. I'm coming to the conclusion that girl really
doesn't know she's alive yet."

"I know what you mean, I think," Monica spoke
thoughtfully, wrinkling her forehead into puzzled
little furrows. "She's, she's—oh I don't know—she's

so terribly correct and right, but she's so often so miserable about it."

"I think that's her trouble. You see, she's tied up with herself. She is a Christian, you can't deny that. She really means what she says she believes, but she isn't one bit liberated. The result is nobody wants her, and she doesn't fit in with folk. Winsome is basing life on all the 'shalts' and 'shalt nots'—and more 'shalt nots' than anything else—and because she's so scared of doing the wrong thing she is critical of others, and that makes them either laugh at her or resent her interference. Nobody really wants the life she lives—she just doesn't commend Christ and His life. That's the tragedy."

"Yes."

Monica's thoughts were back at the beginning of the term. She had gone to St. Adrian's this time full of high hopes and determination to face the foe and triumph. The first few hours had not been very triumphant. Almost at once she had met Winsome Dawlish who had been introduced to her as the new matron for the Junior Girls' House. Monica's heart sank. The stranger before her was obviously shy, ill at ease and yet with an air of doggedness that made her seem almost ruthless when one got to know her better. For the next two hours the two young matrons tried to size each other up. To Monica it was a bitter blow. Of course, she couldn't blame Johnny. After all, she had to remind herself in all honesty, the man had only one's credentials to go on, and hers last year had made her out to be a far keener Chris-

tian than she was. She couldn't blame the Head if
this new matron was not the sort of Christian she
had been counting upon having as a stalwart ally.
She should know that there were Christians and
Christians.

That had been during the afternoon. At tea-time
Pearl had arrived. Johnny had brought her into the
staff room and introduced her all round as the new
senior matron, and had given Monica a specially
meaningful look as he left the staff room to go back
to his own busy affairs. For a while nothing revealed itself. There was small talk, holiday ex-
changes, trivialities. Then the maids arrived carrying the enormous teapots, and tea was poured out.
Monica, hovering near Winsome and Pearl, suddenly
noticed something. Unobtrusively but quite unmis-
takably Pearl had closed her eyes and bowed her
head for quite a few seconds before she started her
tea. Monica's heart leapt. This was more like it.
From that moment the friendship grew, and often
enough it was due to Pearl's quiet steadfastness
that Monica weathered the rough waters of her return to St. Adrian's staff room without shipwreck.
True, Winsome was a Christian as Pearl said, but
something there was missing, and the two friends
tried hard to be patient with her and carry her along
with them as far as she would go.

"Penny for them!" Pearl prodded her companion,
and laughed. "Anyway, here's the bus. Good job
I'm with you, or you would have missed it, standing
there day-dreaming!"

Monica blushed.

"Sorry! I was thinking about the first night of term. I don't think I've ever told you. You know I was here before?" Pearl nodded. There were several speculations about Monica behind her back on the staff. "Well, when Johnny said he would have me back he said he'd got another Christian matron coming. I didn't know Nurse Black had left, and soon after I got back Winsome turned up and I felt awful. I couldn't blame Johnny, because he doesn't know much about keen Christians or dull ones, but I felt all my hopes of real fellowship were shattered. And then you came—and, well, I saw you ask a blessing before you took your tea, and that somehow told me all I needed to know. I was remembering that just now, thinking about Winsome. She's sort of outward in things—I mean, if she thought she ought to say grace in the staff room she'd want everyone to be quiet and tell them they ought to do it too. I can't just fathom her."

"We often can't fathom each other, Monica. That's half our trouble. Half the time we can't fathom ourselves. To me that is always one thing that makes the Fatherhood of God so wonderful. To *know* that in all our foolishness and mistakes and weakness He understands, and He goes on loving us in spite of ourselves."

The bus drew up in the centre of the main shopping area of the town and the two got off, Winsome and her troubles left behind them for the time being.

The day passed swiftly. Christmas shopping was

in the very air. There was only a little more than
six weeks to Christmas now, and already the shops
were alluring with their displays. The busy routine
of term time left little enough leisure for the two
friends to be out together, so they made full use of
the day, going home in the early evening, tired but
well satisfied with their outing.

"Come and have supper in my room, Pearl, will
you?" Monica gave the invitation as the two went
back into the school building.

"I'd love to. Thanks, Monica."

Each matron had a cosy bed-sitting-room, and on
such a day as this in particular they were under no
obligation to spend their evening in the staff room
unless they chose to do so. Pearl arrived at Monica's
door fifteen minutes later and sniffed the air apprecia-
tively.

"Toasted cheese! Scrummy!"

They both laughed.

"I popped into the staff room for my knitting,
Monica, and Winsome is there with Stodge and
Graham Harvey, poor souls, and she is laying down
the law in no mean way about the evils of gambling.
Graham looks mildly amused, and Stodge looks like
a frightened rabbit. I can't think she would know
which end of a horse one should put a shirt on if one
wanted to. It really was priceless. I slipped in without a sound and came away feeling guilty. I couldn't
think if I ought to save Stodge and Graham or bring
Winsome up and deliver her from her own unhappy
self."

D

Monica sighed.

"We ought to have her up, really. Let's just have supper, because she will have had hers, anyway, and then I'll go and rout her out until bedtime. It's so nice just being restful with you and not wondering what argument we shall suddenly find ourselves caught up in, but after all, we've had a jolly decent day. Winsome never seems to have any folk or any letters, and she certainly doesn't make friends easily."

Monica had no difficulty in finding Winsome after supper. The girl was sitting moodily turning the pages of a book in the deserted staff room. Undoubtedly the argument had not finished its course in her favour.

Back in the warmth and friendliness of Monica's room they heard the tiring details. There was a long pause when Winsome had got it all off her chest. Pearl was laboriously counting pattern rows in her knitting, Monica wisely refrained from saying anything that could have started the topic going again. When Pearl had finished she prodded her instructions with a pin to mark where she had got to.

"Everyone is willing to tell us how many shopping days there are before Christmas, but no one ever thinks to tell aunts how many knitting days are left, and the more nephews and nieces one possesses, the shorter the days seem to be. I've this twin set to finish for one niece, a woolly toy for her baby brother, and I promised my other sister I'd knit buster suits for her boys. They are twins, and I don't know, but when you see their neat wee bodies in mid-summer you feel you could knit a dozen minute suits before Christmas—and here I am and only the wool and pattern bought. It's hopeless !''

Suddenly the listless Winsome disappeared and gave way to an eager girl.

"Oh, Pearl, couldn't I help? I just love knitting children's things. Has it a pattern on it?''

Pearl stared. Nothing had so roused enthusiasm in Winsome in such a positive way.

"Why, Winsome, I'd love you to if you've time. Haven't you any work of your own you want to be doing?''

Winsome shook her head.

"I've no nephews or nieces. I've always longed to have some, but I never shall.''

"Well, you'll be more than welcome to knit for Brian and Bobby if you really want to.''

"I do. Honestly, I mean it. I've, well, actually I've no one to be getting anything ready for, and I'd rather be busy.''

Winsome stopped, she had not meant to say so much. She went back to the subject on hand.

"Have you the wool with you? I could start to-night.''

Pearl realised that Winsome was in earnest. Laying down her work, she got up.

"I won't be a sec.; I'll get it. I shall be awfully pleased to get it done, Winsome.''

The two smiled at each other. The one as grateful for the chance to do something as the other to have it done.

Monica sat staring into the fire. She had fetched
out a tea-cloth she was embroidering for Aunt Mollie.
So Winsome had no one to be making Christmas
plans for. She thought back to her childhood. Glendorran had buzzed with girls buying presents to take
home, girls hurriedly knitting socks for brothers and
fathers, scarfs and gloves for mothers. Much of it
had been weird and wonderful, especially in her
earliest years there, but it had been THE thing one
did in the winter term, and she had always felt left
out. Aunt Mollie and Uncle James would not have
known how to accept a childish offering. She would
be given money when she got home and would go
and buy some worthless trinket for her aunt and
some expensive trifle for her uncle. Her parents
in their dim and remote equatorial home would not
appreciate anything knitted. She could understand
Winsome better now. She wondered about her. Had
she no one, just no one that cared?

When Pearl rejoined them and had unfolded the
pattern and Winsome had gone into raptures over
the pretty colours and the soft wool, Monica made
a very deliberate move.

"What plans for Christmas, you two?" she asked,
carefully avoiding Pearl's glance.

There was a moment's silence.

Winsome coloured and bent over the stitches she
was casting on. Pearl considered the matter before
she spoke.

"I hardly know. Mummy and Daddy are abroad,
of course. Ever since we children came home each

Christmas seems to have been different. At first we all went to Granny's from school, and then Granny died and I used to try to herd the younger ones together, even if only for the two or three days. Just once Mummy and Daddy managed a Christmas at home—that was the year I left school. Since then, well, I was usually at hospital. It's a busy time and not easy to get leave then, and once I was fully trained I really came straight here after I'd done a bit of general nursing. Both my young sisters are married, but one is in the very north of Scotland and the other in Cornwall, so there's not much hope of a family reunion. The boys are busy with their own affairs, too, this year. What about you, Monica?''

Monica cut the thread she was using and laid it aside. Picking up a length of soft green silk, she rethreaded her needle before she spoke.

"Well, I've got about the greatest good fortune anyone could have. You may not know that I went to school at Glendorran. It's a smashing Christian school, and you meet a wonderful crowd there; the staff are Christians and lots of the girls, especially the older ones. Well, my Aunt Mollie was there too, and there's a friend of hers who was also there—she's married to a Sir Christopher Cardinal, and they've a gorgeous place in Surrey. They are going to give their big house, a Manor House, over to training children after polio and that sort of thing, but for this last Christmas they are going to have a really super house-party there—all the old crowd from Glendorran—a generation before me—my aunt's crowd, and I was there in the summer, so Lady Cardinal has invited me, too.''

"How nice, Monica, I am glad!'' Pearl interrupted Monica's exultant flow.

"You be quiet! That's not all. I was going to tell you tonight, Pearl, only this is a much better chance. I can take two friends with me, so what about coming to Cobleigh? What about you, Winsome? Would that bust up any plan of yours?''

For a moment there was no answer, and Winsome did not lift her head from her work. When she did Monica and Pearl were surprised by an altogether new look in her eyes, and there was a suspicion of something very like a tear.

"Monica, are you sure? I mean, you're not just asking because I said I wasn't making anything for anyone?''

"My dear child, listen, I only got the letter this morning, and I've just been turning it over in my mind and praying about it all day. I haven't even told Pearl until now. When you said about not having anyone to make preparations for I remembered my own Christmas holidays. As a school kid I loathed them. My parents were abroad, and the aunt and uncle I went to were terribly social and unhomely. I was bored and miserable with them, and they, poor dears, must have been thankful when the holidays were over. I just thought maybe I wouldn't be tearing you away from the bosom of the family from the way you spoke.''

There was always something attractive and

friendly about Monica, and now, without warning, Winsome's carefully built defences were suddenly down. In the warm and kindly atmosphere she opened up to the two who really wanted to be friends with her and who had tried often enough to help her.

"No, I've no family bosom to be torn from. You see, I don't remember a home or a family. I grew up in an orphanage. It was a jolly good orphanage —a Christian one—and I'm jolly proud of it. The folk are dears, and I can always go back there, but the staff change, and the children change, and the busy life goes on without you between whiles, and somehow, with all they do it never really seems home when you go back after the first year or two."

Pearl and Monica went on silently with their work. Now that the floodgates were open it was good just to let Winsome ramble on. All the time the two listeners were weighing up all that they knew of her and feeling that in all this background lay a good many of the answers to her problems. When she stopped, Pearl, whose experience of people was more mature than Monica's, asked Winsome a question.

"Did you come to the Lord in the Home?"

"Yes."

"Tell us about it, won't you?"

There was a kind and keenly interested note in Pearl's voice.

"There's not much to tell. We had quite a lot of prayers and services, and sometimes on Sunday nights we had special speakers. I was quite small at

the time, but I remember a man coming and telling
us about Jesus and His love, and then he said
wouldn't we like to ask Jesus to be our Saviour and
to give us a new heart, and if we would to stand up.
I stood up. Oh, I suppose I was about seven or
eight, then, Pearl.'' Winsome stopped in the nar-
rative to answer her friend's question. ''After that
the staff made quite a fuss of me for a bit, and then
some of them seemed to expect much more of me—
you know, being good and all that because of what
I'd done. But what puzzled me so much was that I
was the only one who stood up. I never could understand it. The way he put it I thought everyone would,
and really I only stood because I was afraid I'd be
the only one who didn't.''

There was a very tender, motherly look in Pearl's
eyes as she reached out a hand and took hold of
Winsome's. During the telling of her tale the girl
had been fidgeting nervously. Pearl saw a great deal
in that simple telling.

''Winsome, my dear, I want to tell you something
which I think may help you because I was once at a
meeting—I was a much older Christian and the same
thing happened. It was a Nurses' Christian Fellowship, and we had a wonderful talk from a doctor
home from a leper colony. At the end he gave an
opportunity for anyone who had not come to Christ
to come, and one or two nurses did, but then he
gave another appeal. He spoke to those of us already
the Lord's—I can remember his words to this day.
He said, 'if you are willing by His grace to let Him

put you where He wants you for the rest of your lives, in this or any other country, as we bow our heads will you silently stand in your places'. To me that seemed the simplest of requests, and one which simply could not be refused. As you say, fearing lest I should be alone in my seat, I sprang up at once. There were about thirty in that meeting and, my dear, three of us stood to that appeal. I know exactly how you felt, and I am not going to attempt to explain it. I can only say that the Holy Spirit works in hearts that are willing to be worked in, and we do not realise it—we simply know we must obey. Don't worry about those to whom the appeal meant nothing, just be thankful that when He called *you* you were listening and you answered. Almost everything about our salvation, as about so much of Christian life will remain a mystery for us to the end of our days because God's ways are so much more wonderful than our own, but I've learnt one thing which has helped me so much. Somebody once said this to me: 'God does not ask us to be Understanders, only Believers.' Accept the fact that in His grace and mercy He apprehended you for Himself and you responded, and remember that is only the beginning. The true Christian life goes on getting more and more a matter of liberation and joy and 'perfect freedom' in Christ. Press on, Winsome, and don't let yourself be narrowed down to too legal a view—remember He came to give us life more abundant. When people see us with boundless joy and peace, no matter what is going on, they begin

to want to know what we've got and where we get it
from. And now, Pearl Adams, stop preaching a ser-
mon, you are making mistakes in your knitting!''

Pearl's remark and the laugh it raised broke the
very serious atmosphere that the evening's talking
had produced. Presently Winsome slipped away, a
happier Winsome than St. Adrian's had so far seen.

As Pearl gathered up her knitting and prepared to
say good night to Monica she spoke of Winsome
again.

''You know, I think all that may be the explanation of Winsome. Poor child, she's not got an easy
background, and you see her very start as a Christian was tied up with 'oughts' and 'ought nots'. I
honestly believe tonight may be the beginning of a
new lease of really spiritual life for her. Wouldn't
that be wonderfully worthwhile? And, Monica, about
Cobleigh, are you sure we could come? It would be
simply marvellous. I didn't know you had been at
Glendorran. Our best two nurses my year, and the
keenest Christians—in fact the other two who stood
when I did—were Glendorrians. We thought a lot of
them. One is in a leper colony already, and the other
is making the same act of obedience, but at home,
caring for a suddenly widowed and ill father. The
two had hoped to go out together.''

The friends separated, and before Monica settled
for bed she wrote to Wendy thanking her for the invitation and accepting most gratefully for herself
and Pearl and Winsome.

CHAPTER ELEVEN

CHRISTMAS AT COBLEIGH

THE term finished with a flourish at St. Adrian's on December 18th. Never were Junior Dormitories and the Sick Bay put to rights so quickly. By mid-morning on the 19th Monica and her two friends had thrown aside the shackles of matrondom and were as free as the boys and girls who had gone home the previous day.

The first stage of their journey took them to London, and there they stayed for the night and the next day, entering into the gaiety of the season and doing their last-minute Christmas shopping.

Pearl was her usual happy self. Hers was an even sort of temperament which did not readily fluctuate; she could join wholeheartedly into whatever she might be doing with others. Winsome was still unfolding day by day. Ever since that evening in Monica's room at half-term the two friends had been finding out that there was another Winsome beneath the rather troubled, anxious exterior—a Winsome who could be great fun and who seemed to blossom out in the kindness of their jolly companionship. Monica, too, was eagerly entering into all that was going on, but at the back of her mind she was carrying a weighty problem which baffled her.

Just a few days before the school had broken up she had found a letter and gift waiting for her from Uncle James, and that had started an old train of thought. If only he and Aunt Mollie would try to make a new beginning. She loved them both, and it was miserable the way this business kept them apart. Perhaps at Cobleigh Mrs. Summers might still be there. Perhaps she could ask her. She wondered if that would be fair on Aunt Mollie. She wondered about asking her aunt, but felt she wouldn't like to. The two were much closer now than they used to be, but Aunt Mollie's relationship with Uncle James was a sticky subject for a young niece to touch upon.

By the time the three reached Cobleigh the following evening they were in the highest of spirits and ready to join all the fun that was going on. The house already seemed to be filled to capacity, but although so many were strangers to each other, by the end of the first riotous and happy evening they were all very much at home together.

With still four days to Christmas Eve the whole household found plenty to do. There was a sharp frost and a touch of light snow on the ground. There was holly to cut for decorations, logs to stack beside the wide-open hearth, and everywhere the house rang with merry voices and the sound of busy, hurrying feet.

The old Dormy crowd—June, Edna, Janet, Mollie —were sleeping together in a small room on the first floor, and it was on the second night, leaning out of the window drinking in the wonder of the sparkling world, that June was suddenly struck by a streak of wild mischief. Calling the others excitedly to her, she pointed from their window. Below them was a flat lead roof at a drop of less than three feet. Beyond was the low roof of the single-storey room in which, for the holiday, the three from St. Adrian's were housed. Near to the flat roof was the short, disused chimney-stack that led to the fireplace in that room.

"Let's have some fun," June whispered to the others. "I saw a smashing piece of chain in the stable. Let's tie a bell on to the end and clank the thing down the chimney."

All decorum, as befitted their age, had gone to the winds. Giggling like schoolgirls, they crept back to bed and laid their plans.

During the next day they tried hard not to give themselves away. Janet had carefully got herself invited into the room and had seen how the land lay. Pearl's bed was nearest the fireplace, and while all the guests were busy after dinner in the sitting-room, she had slipped the chain and an old hand-bell up to their room.

When all was quiet and in darkness the four friends softly pushed up the window.

"We are a crazy gang! Anyone would think we were in our teens!"

Janet, helping June into an old pair of dungarees, was not really in the least stand-offish, but heartily enjoying the fun. With a lot of giggling and muffled whispers, June was eased out over the sill and on to the flat roof. Then Edna handed out the chain, and finally the bell. Already they had wired it round the handle and tied a hook on to the chain to link the two together.

"Good hunting, June!" breathed the waiting trio. "Don't forget to take the cotton-wool out of the bell when you get there, or it won't ring!"

From the darkened window they watched June's stealthy movements silhouetted against the pale light of the moon. Down in the room below all was quiet. The three had put out the light, lain for a while talking softly until first one and then another had dropped off to sleep. Only Monica lay awake. Mostly the days were too busy now to allow of her brooding over her problem, but all the same, sooner or later it had to be faced, and once Christmas was over she would have no excuse at all to keep her from writing to Uncle James in answer to his letter and Christmas present.

She turned over. She wanted to get to sleep and yet, somehow, there was something rather good about being drowsily awake when everyone else was asleep. These were such happy days. Sometimes she felt as if life passed so swiftly that one never seemed to have time to take hold of the happy things and really enjoy them. Suddenly she stiffened. What was that? A bell. She lay and listened. It wasn't the 'phone or the front door. It was too near for the church. Oh, it couldn't be a fire-bell, surely? Springing out of bed, she roused Pearl. Winsome woke at the disturbance. Clang! Clang! It sounded terribly near. They all listened.

"The wind must have got up." Pearl tried to speak reassuringly. "I expect there's an outside bell—on some old coach-house—that we haven't noticed, and I expect the wind has caught it."

At that moment there was a terrific clatter and a thud, obviously very near to their room. Instantly the three struggled into slippers and dressing gowns. Was it fire? Or was someone trying to break in? They opened the door cautiously and peered out into the dark hall and corridors. They waited, huddled together. There was no smell of smoke, no sound of fire, no sound of anything at all. Nothing to see. They went back into their room and turned up the light.

"I think the sensible thing would be to take our torches and just go quietly round the house." Pearl looked at her watch. "It's only one o'clock. No burglar would do anything that made a bell ring, and if he did he wouldn't wait around to see what happened next. I can't see any point in waking the family unless we find anything wrong. Game?"

The other two agreed. They didn't mind what they did if they were all doing it together with plenty of lights on. Out they trooped, turning on the hall light. They crept quietly through room after room and then went upstairs, making no sound, and only listening to see that all was well within the occupied rooms. Satisfied that no one was in trouble and that there was no evidence of disaster, they went back to

bed but not to sleep. For a while the three curled up
in Pearl's bed at her companionable suggestion, and
feasted on biscuits and fruit until they began to feel
sleepy. Then they went back to their own beds, and
soon nothing could be heard but the long, deep, even
breathing that told they were all asleep.

With the coming of the morning they tried to remember what it was that had happened, and why it
was that they felt as if they had hardly been to bed
at all. Then they remembered.

Over the breakfast bacon and egg they recounted
their night's adventure. The household seemed quite
impressed, but only to the extent of suggesting that
there were cures for indigestion and that the three
had better go to bed early in future instead of being
up so late. Pearl gingerly kicked Monica's foot. When
she caught her eye she nodded in June's direction.
Monica looked across at the girl sitting obliquely
from her. June was obviously trying to bury her
sense of humour in a slice of toast and butter. Janet
was very preoccupied with a cup of tea. Edna seemed
to have dropped her handkerchief, and by the time
she had stooped and fished about for it, her face was
very red.

"We'll get to the bottom of this, yet," Pearl de-
clared after breakfast. "If that crowd doesn't know
something about it I'm going to be jolly surprised!"

"I guess they know all there is to know!" Winsome joined in. "Did you see Edna's face?"

"I did," Pearl said drily.

The four friends were not really as easy in their

minds as they tried to seem. They had a small but
rather important matter to see to that morning. A
good length of chain and a very nice handbell had
got to be put back where they had been found and,
at the moment, that was quite an impossible feat.
The night before, just when everything was going
well, June had to make a sudden decision. Either
she must let go and tumble off the roof or save herself and let go the chain and bell. She had the good
sense to save herself, and her feet, which had begun
to slip came to rest miraculously on the guttering.
Crestfallen, she had crept back to the others. The
bell and the chain had gone rattling out of reach
down the chimney, and June knew that the chimney
was blocked up at the bottom.

Feeling very much like ridiculously naughty children, the four made their way to their host's study,
full of apologies, but it was Christmas, and Christopher only threw his head back and roared at the
escapade, though he had to admit that it was not the
sort of thing he had foreseen from this particular
batch of guests.

"Still," he said good-naturedly, "no bones were
broken and the trio downstairs don't seem to have
been unduly alarmed, but, wait a minute—that re-
minds me—I know what I'll do with the lot of you.
You can jolly well report yourselves to Andy and
Wendy in public after dinner tonight—in fact to all
the staff and ex-staff of Glendorran; maybe that
will teach you that discretion is the much better part
of valour!"

The four were dismissed with a smile, but Christopher kept them to it and that night after dinner, in an uproarious scene well planned by himself, they had to appear before Andy, Wendy, Miss Bridger, and Miss Carpenter, brought in by a very fierce-looking Lindsey in the old-fashioned dress of a School Nurse.

And then, the carols started and suddenly in the midst of all the fun Christmas was on them. Outside on the clear, frosty air came the music of the boys of the Estate, then girls' voices took up the notes. The Manor doors were flung open, and the guests rushed for warm coats and scarves and streamed out into the night to join the singers as they went on their way to sing outside the homes of the old people.

For three days the festivities went on. Much of the time was spent in quietly enjoying each other's company, for in that atmosphere it was easy to make friendships that lasted, to talk quietly over the things that matter most and to find ways and means of helping and being helped together to live that life which, but for the first Christmas, could never have been lived by mortal man.

It was during the long, quiet hours that Monica got her opportunity. Just once she found herself in the room alone with Andy. Could she speak of it? Was this the time? All at once it was easy, easy as Andy always made it easy for a girl to unburden herself of any trouble or pressing problem that needed to be shared.

Monica took the plunge. "And what about Aunt

Mollie? Would it be fair to talk to her, I mean? You see, it's difficult about her. When she first came to the Lord, Uncle James just scoffed, but after a bit he used to ask me, when he saw me, how things were going, and he didn't scoff. He just seemed to be waiting for something. Ever since I've been old enough to understand what salvation means—even before I made a mess of things at St. Adrian's—I used to feel badly about Aunt Mollie and Uncle James. I know he's watching to see what she makes of being a Christian, but Aunt Mollie is so different about him. She has just written off the whole marriage as a big mistake in her life, accepts the fact that God has saved her from it—I mean as well as saved her from sin and all that—delivered her from that mistake. Now, to her, Uncle James just belongs to the old life—a closed chapter—and is nothing more to do with her. I used to feel miserable about it, though I didn't know why, but after you talked to me about marriage in the summer I've felt even worse! I'm not mad with Aunt Mollie exactly, but just sort of grieved somewhere inside—I can't explain.''

"No, my dear, I'm sure you can't, but I understand. It's one of those things we can do nothing to interfere with ourselves, but we can and we must pray. You can do that, and so can I. There is nothing impossible with God—always remember that—and couples who have become estranged do get back together again 'in Christ'. So long as you just keep your own steadfast walk with the Lord down to these little details they will bear a brighter, clearer testimony than if you set yourself to tell either of them what you think they ought to do, however right you might happen to be."

"Oh, Mrs. Summers, you are a comfort!"

At that moment others came and joined them, but Monica had her answer and was satisfied. Her letter to Uncle James was not an easy one to write, but once done, she felt better able to enjoy the rest of the holiday.

CHAPTER TWELVE

REUNION

MONICA was busy packing her small suitcase. The
holiday was over. Already Pearl had left to visit
a brother on the way back to school, and she had
taken Winsome with her. Most of the older guests,
too, had gone, and in another hour she would be saying her good-byes and catching the train that would
start her on the first part of her journey back to St.
Adrian's. There was a knock at the door.

"Come in!"

It was Wendy.

"May I come in for a minute? Good! Monica,
we've been talking, Christopher and Andy and I,
and we wondered just how you were feeling about
St. Adrian's now. You see, with the expansion here
the staff will have to be increased. I spoke to Lindsey
about making arrangements for that, and she has
begged me to have a word with you. What do you
think? It need not be till after Easter—you would
need to work this term out, but we'd love to have
you here with the children."

Monica stood looking at Wendy. This was terrific.
To be offered a job here in Cobleigh with June and
Lindsey and with these children who so needed
Christian help. She pulled herself up quickly. Win-

some flashed into her mind. Then the dormitory with its fifteen blue beds and their trim blue-and-white counterpanes—trim until fifteen small boys made havoc of the place, as they did every evening. Then she thought of the fifteen small boys. They needed Christian help, too. Of course, they'd get it in the sick bay, but the standard of health at St. Adrian's was high, and the boys did not frequent the sick bay. She turned gravely to her friend.

"Wendy, it's the most—most stupendous suggestion. I suppose I ought to say I'd like time to think about it, but really and truly I'd rather not; I'd rather decide now, because I do know where I ought to be—at St. Adrian's. The kiddies here will get loads of help, but if I quit St. Adrian's there's nobody for those little chaps. Pearl only gets them if they're sick, and Winsome gets the girls. I've fifteen small boys, and you know, most of them seem to get nothing at home to really stand by them. Just one or two expect to say their prayers when they first come—but they are in the minority I'm afraid. And then there's Winsome. No, I'd love to come but—well, that's how things are."

"I know. And, Monica, take this bit of comfort back with you. I, too, couldn't help seeing what a happy plan it might be for us all if you came to us, but in my heart of hearts this is the answer I rather hoped you'd give."

Wendy left her alone then, and the girl went back to her packing with a new sense of encouragement. So Wendy thought she had done right! Her heart

warmed as she strapped her case. Then it was time
to go out to the others and drink a cup of coffee before her journey, and say good-bye.

Back at St. Adrian's she was swiftly caught into
all the excitement and busy life of school. Boys'
clothes to sort and mend and patch, boys' necks and
knees to wash, their minor bumps and bruises to
heal, their little hurts and troubles to heed and help.
And Monica loved every minute of it. Off duty she
usually managed to see something of Pearl, or Winsome, or both, and the term flowed evenly on its
way with an average proportion of wet days and
cancelled matches, and sudden bursts of spring sunshine that made them fling all the windows joyfully
wide open.

Half-term in the January term was something of a
special occasion at St. Adrian's. It usually coincided
very nearly with Founder's Day, and so the Friday
was always set aside as a great event to which parents
and friends were invited and at which the children
did their best to shine for the sake of the school.
Being around the end of February and the beginning
of March, it was never safe to plan an outdoor pro-
gramme, but the children gave a display in the gym-
nasium in the morning and a concert in the afternoon, and St. Adrian's Founder's Day was known
to be of a high standard.

Monica had her hands more than full. All her fifteen boys were doing something, and as it was their
first Founder's Day they were keyed up to a high
pitch of excitement. There were parents to meet,

with all that that means for the matron who really
bothers to pay heed to what a small boy's mother
has to say about her son or ask about his own particular ways and behaviour. And all the time Monica
had an uneasy feeling, a little excitement of her very
own that could thrill her one minute and then make
her fearful the next. Talking to the parents, she gave
them every possible scrap of her attention, but all
the time her eyes were apt to roam over the rapidly
thickening crowd coming into the hall searching for
two faces. And then she saw them, suddenly, un-
expectedly, and to her utter amazement they were
together, not only together, but arm in arm and
looking as if they liked it. Uncle James and Aunt
Mollie! Monica waved frantically, and was immediately swamped by more parents and had to fight
back her longing to get to the bottom of the mystery.
True, it was exactly what she had hoped might happen before the day was out. That was why she had
written to each of them quite separately, never men-
tioning the other, and invited each to be her guest
at St. Adrian's Founder's Day. Never had she
dreamt of them coming together, and she was all
impatience to know how it had come about.

After the gym display the visitors were served
with a cold buffet lunch in the hall and the children
had their own lunch in the play-room. Then, still
without time to talk, there was the tuning up of the
school orchestra, the signal that the concert was
about to begin. Monica managed to slip up behind
her aunt and uncle when she had located them and

to have a brief word with them, but they obviously did not need to be entertained.

"You young monkey!" Uncle James twinkled at her. "Can you come out to dinner tonight? That seems our only hope of a proper talk, and we need to have a celebration, you know."

Monica promised to try, and one glance at Aunt Mollie told her that this was indeed a very happy day worth celebrating.

At last the festivities were over, the boys, except those who had already gone home with their parents for the rest of the half-term holiday, in bed and sound asleep. Monica slipped into a pretty dress and went off to find her relatives.

"Now who's going to talk first, I want to hear everything?"

Monica sat back comfortably, thoroughly prepared to enjoy her evening out.

"Well, today's event seemed to hinge on your cunningly devised plan to bring your wicked old uncle and your aunt to a meeting-place—but you see, Monica, the whole thing got taken out of your hands. Now listen carefully, because this is going to take a bit of believing, only Mollie here can vouch for the truth of it. I got your letter and turned the thing down as out of the question. I expected to be in Paris today. Then all those plans fell through—nothing to do with me at all—and late last night I found myself with this whole week-end utterly free, and I got a sudden desire to come and see you and St. Adrian's, so I just packed my suitcase and came. I had plenty of time, found a nice compartment and settled down to the paper. We were nearly due to leave when I looked up. People were hurrying along the platform by then, and I just noticed one face—'how like what Mollie used to be, that woman is' I thought, and at that moment the train whistle blew and a porter flung open our door and helped that very lady in.''

"And it was Aunt Mollie? Whatever did you do?'' Monica giggled.

Her two elders laughed.

"You may well ask, Monica. I took one look at James and fell completely in love with him. Oh, I know that sounds mushy, but it's perfectly true. As soon as I saw James I realised what I had been doing. I had been putting our marriage as the thing which belonged to the old life and could not be carried into the new, whereas this morning I suddenly saw that it was the drifting apart, the breakdown of our marriage that could not go on, the marriage itself had to be recovered by the Lord and for the Lord.''

"And with His help it shall be, my dear. But let me tell Monica my bit of the story. She deserves to know. After Christmas she wrote me a quiet, kind, friendly little letter that warmed my lonely old heart. But what she did not know was that for months I had been feeling uncomfortable about something. When Mollie first became converted I was cynical, I'll admit it. It was as good a craze as any she had indulged in, and it wasn't likely to last any longer than the rest. But it wasn't a craze, and it did last.

I began to get interested in the God who could tame Mollie Ridelle. That was the God I had learnt about as a boy, a great God who knew nothing of impossibilities. I had let that vision of God get hidden under the semi-fashionable god of nominal religion until at last He had been dethroned altogether by the gods of this world. But as I heard about Mollie's steady progress I began to get uneasy. I would have liked to get in touch with her again, but to go to her and seek to win her back touched my pride. To follow my wife into full Christian living would mean radical changes in my whole way of life.''

Uncle James paused. It was not too easy to tell these intimate things to Monica, and yet, somehow, she seemed more of a contemporary than a youngster. Age didn't seem to be the chief concern.

"So?" Monica was following breathlessly.

Uncle James smiled.

"Again, almost unbelievably unless you believe in the God of wonderful things, I met a fine man on the Continent and realised he was a man of great worth—not worldly worth but what I needed. I was right. He was splendid, and he spent hours helping me and showing me the right path back to God, and then we prayed together. Of course my pride suffered, but what did that matter when I had learnt to call it by its right name—sin? And now I am free, utterly free to begin again, and utterly thankful to God that my wife is willing to begin again with me.

Soon after dinner Monica had to go back to school,

but she left behind her the happiest couple she had ever seen, and as she let herself into her room that night she was remembering all the wise and good things she had discovered at Cobleigh and which had helped her to want Aunt Mollie and Uncle James to come together again.